D0788999

Large Print Western OLSEN
Theodore
Olsen, Theodore V.
Blood of the breed [text (large
print)]

Good book

BLOOD OF THE BREED

Center Point
Large Print

Also by T. V. Olsen and available from
Center Point Large Print:

Bonner's Stallion

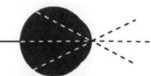

BLOOD OF THE BREED

T. V. OLSEN

CENTER POINT LARGE PRINT
THORNDIKE, MAINE

This Center Point Large Print edition
is published in the year 2013 by arrangement with
Golden West Literary Agency.

Copyright © 1982 by T. V. Olsen.

All rights reserved.

The text of this Large Print edition is unabridged.
In other aspects, this book may vary
from the original edition.
Printed in the United States of America
on permanent paper.
Set in 16-point Times New Roman type.

ISBN: 978-1-61173-685-4

Library of Congress Cataloging-in-Publication Data

Olsen, Theodore V.
  Blood of the breed / T. V. Olsen.
  pages ; cm.
  ISBN 978-1-61173-685-4 (library binding : alk. paper)
  1. Large type books. I. Title.
  PS3565.L8B5 2013
  813'.54—dc23
                                        2012042241

To "Moms" Butler
from "Sunny" Law

BLOOD OF THE BREED

CHAPTER 1

Once a year Nathan Drew rode up the flank of a long sloping meadow deep on Swallowtail's top range.

He followed the traces of a road that only faintly showed here and there because it was hardly ever used. A good thirty years ago, a team-drawn scraper had leveled the roughest spots along the several miles of high country range that lay between Swallowtail's headquarters and its little cemetery. The earth scars were long overgrown, but you could still make them out, and a spring wagon could follow them on the occasional times that it served as a hearse.

How many times had he followed such a procession along this route? Idly, as he rode up the long stretch of meadow on this bright morning, Nathan Drew tried to recall how often.

Ten times? A dozen? No more than a dozen, he decided, during the twenty-two years he had lived on Swallowtail. Ranch people died like anyone else, but outside of the family, not a lot of them died in the ranch's service unless it was with their boots on.

The meadow tilted sharply across the lift of a ridge, and just beyond was the burying ground. It lay on a high knoll that overlooked a vast sweep of pine timber and summer-cured grass that dropped away in easy terraces to the north and west.

Nathan pulled up his piebald horse and gazed across the panoramic fallaway of land. It was quite a view, all right. That's why Aunt Lu had insisted that the ranch cemetery be located at this point. Ike Banner liked to tell how he had brought his bride up here soon after they were married. He'd hoped to impress her with exactly this view, and Luella had been ecstatic. But Ike had been dismayed when she'd come up with the enthusiastic notion of reserving this knoll as a last resting place for Swallowtail people. Now, more than thirty years later, Ike could chuckle over the memory. But knowing how crotchety he could still get—although Ike had mellowed a good deal with the years—Nathan could guess that the occasion had sparked some pretty heated words between the newlyweds. Aunt Lu, for all her soft and gentle ways, had had a mind like a steel trap. Once it snapped onto an idea, a man lief as try to budge a mountain.

"By God, I tell you now," Ike would say, laughing and slapping his knee, "if that woman didn't get the damnedest ideas! Like naming this man's ranch 'Swallowtail.' I mean, Jesus, can you feature a working outfit with a sissy handle like *that?* I wanted to call the place Cross B. Jesus! A man puts all he's got, savings and sweat and blood, into developing a spread like this one.

And then the slip of a girl he's married wants to put frills on it! Well, by God, that's just what Luella went and done. Put frills on about everything but me. I was too mean to change. Oh, and she was shrewd, that woman! Knew just how far she could go with a man and never tried for an inch more. Well, it didn't matter that by God this piece of ground was miles from the headquarters and we would have a hell of a time making a road to it. 'It is a lovely place, Isaac,' says she. 'I can think of no place more fitting to lay our loved ones to rest when their time comes.' That's how she wanted it and that's how it's been. There has been a fair share of people planted on that knoll since then."

Nathan's straight mouth held the hint of a smile as he swung down from his saddle. He could picture how Aunt Lu had looked and sounded when she informed her husband of how it was going to be. Ike hated his full Christian name, and Luella had never addressed him by it except when she was riding herd on something she'd set her heart on. Once she did, a body could pretty well conclude that Ike's battle was lost.

Throwing his reins, Nathan Drew walked toward the back of the small burying lot. Grass grew rank and deep around the less than twenty wooden markers that studded the knoll. All of them were nicely fashioned of good solid hardwood. The names and dates (when known) of the deceased were chiseled or burned by hot iron into the wood. Several of the headboards were hard onto three decades old, while the most recent one had been set in place last year. You could single out the oldest ones by what time and weather had done to them, but even these had held up well over the years.

At a far rear corner of the lot, Nathan pulled up in front of a pair of gray, seamed headboards. Since his last visit here, just a year ago, the grass and weeds had grown so thickly around the two markers they were almost hidden.

It was almost noon; the sun was high and hot against Nathan's back. As he dropped to one knee and tugged off his hat, he pulled the sleeve of his faded calico shirt across his forehead, wiping away sweat. He scrubbed a hand over his jaw and stared at the firmly carved letters on the left-hand headboard:

Angus Drew
1821–1868
A Son of Scotland

It was a twin of the other, more recent marker, which had been put up a decade and a half ago:

Horse Woman
d. 1875
Wife of Angus Drew

12

Horse Woman. Not Ma's true Navajo name, but as near as you could put it in English. Maybe it was fitting, at that. Over the last seven years of her life, she had been "Horse Woman" to everyone at Swallowtail. And she hadn't really had much to do with her own people any longer.

Without thinking about it, Nathan Drew began pulling up weeds and throwing them to one side, clearing away the ground around the two markers. Whenever he came to this place, he tried never to think very much about things. It never did any good. He only came here out of a sense of duty.

If it bothered him so much, he sometimes wondered, why do it at all?

Maybe because even a half-breed needed a feel of his roots. Of an origin and a belonging. As his friend Diego Cruz had told him, "If a man ain't one thing or the other, *amigo*, he had better just take the best from both. That's all he can do. What else is there?"

What else? Not a hell of a lot. And Nathan had tried, for sure. Most ways, he figured, he hadn't done too badly. Maybe that was his part of the tough-bitten independence that had led Angus Drew to run away from home, from his native Scotland, at fifteen and take a sailing ship to America. The same fierce independence that had led Angus Drew into the far West and the free, wild life of the old-time mountain men.

It was a streak of good toughness for a man to

have in him. Gave him a sense of his own worth as a man. Nathan spent very little time brooding about the way of things. It rarely bothered him much except on his rare visits to where his father and mother were buried.

But it did trouble him then. Reminded him with a quick, hurting poignancy that he was different, after all. Something like that marked a man deep inside where nobody else could see. And when he got pondering on it, it hurt.

So he pushed the thoughts out of his head, letting his hands busy themselves with yanking out and tossing aside a clutter of weeds from around the weather-stained headboards. After a couple minutes, though, his hands grew still. He stared musingly at his father's grave.

I can't remember much of what he was like, Nathan thought. *I can hardly remember him at all.*

Six years old. He had been six when Angus Drew, stricken by pneumonia, had wheezed his life away in a Navajo hogan. Shortly afterward, Horse Woman had brought her young son to Swallowtail and a different way of life. Shouldn't six be old enough to remember more in the way of details? Yet all that Nathan could recall with any certainty about his father were his striking mops of flaming red hair and beard. And those final days in which Angus Drew had slowly coughed himself to death.

Not much for a man to hold in memory. His father's tough, independent streak was something that Nathan took for granted from what his mother had told him, long ago. And from what Ike Banner, who'd been Angus Drew's next-to-closest friend, had told him in recent times. . . .

Nathan straightened up from his task. He clamped his sweat-stained hat back on his head. He was done here. Might as well be gone.

Standing erect, Nathan Drew was not a tall man. His trunk was thick and stocky, deep-chested and wide-shouldered. He was built along compact lines, yet heavily muscled in a way that suggested both strength and agility. His Indian heritage was overpowering; hardly a trace of the white showed. His hair was straight and ink-black, coarse as a mule's mane. His face was square and flat, brown as a coffee bean, the mouth as tight as a seam. And he never showed much of anything, no matter what he thought.

Like a lot of half-bloods, he could have passed for years to either side of his actual age, which was twenty-eight.

He wore the rough clothes of any working puncher. The only touch that set off his appearance was a bright beaded belt of Navajo workmanship. It was decorated with silver conches and supported a fine sheath of tooled leather. This held a long grooved dagger—not a knife—with a bone hilt that was ornately inset with silver and lapis lazuli.

Nathan cherished that dagger. He wore it like a talisman. In a way, maybe that's what it was. It had been a gift from his mother's father, who'd been a Navajo shaman.

Briefly, his glance passed across the other grave markers.

Maybe a baker's dozen of them identified crewmen who had died, one way or the other, in Swallowtail's service. But four of them marked the burials of children, two boys and two girls, who had been born to Ike and Luella Banner over the years. None of these had survived past the age of two. But three sons had lived and grown to manhood: the legacy of a stormy and yet incredibly happy marriage.

Nathan's gaze sought the wooden slab over the grave of Luella Banner. Momentarily his thoughts softened. After the death of Horse Woman, Ike's wife had taken over the raising of the thirteen-year-old Nathan as if he were one of her own. Aunt Lu had been in her own grave (the gravesite she had chosen so long ago) for more than two years. Yet Nathan Drew remembered her as vividly as yesterday: a bustling, apple-cheeked dumpling of a woman, starched and smiling, with kind eyes that had found life good. A goodness that fed itself out to everyone around her.

In that memory, there was no pain or confusion. In Nathan's own mind at first, and later in direct address, he had shyly called her "Aunt Lu." And his memories of her were warmer and better than those of his true mother, who had been as brusque and distant as she'd been dutiful. Horse Woman had wasted no real liking on her only son. He had never known why. . . .

Well, he had better things to do than stand around here making memories.

Nathan walked back to the piebald, picked up his reins and stepped into the saddle. Quartering the animal around, he followed the sloping meadow downward. But not back the way he had come, along the old road trace to headquarters. Instead, he lifted the piebald into a brisk pace due west.

The trip to his parents' graves was a side reason for his being way up on Swallowtail's north range. Ike had asked him to pay a call on the Purleys—father and two sons—who held down a remote line camp on the far northwest section. Ike hadn't spelled out just what he wanted him to look for, but Nathan knew the old man had no liking or trust for the trio. It was a feeling that Nathan shared, and Ike knew it.

Trouble was, Ike couldn't follow up his private feelings more outwardly without seeming to cast doubt on the judgment of Thorp, his oldest son and foreman. Thorp Banner had charge of the hiring and firing done on Swallowtail. He'd hired the Purleys and had assigned them to that line shack. Thorp was a big, outspoken man with a temper, and his pa didn't want a falling out with him over ranch personnel. Nathan was to have a casual look around the camp and report back to Ike himself.

Nathan reflected that he and Ike had quite a few confidential, almost unspoken arrangements of that sort. It gave him a quiet pleasure that Ike depended on him in small ways, situations in which he couldn't look to any of his sons for help. Officially, Nathan Drew was Swallowtail's resident horsebreaker. Privately, and over a period of years, he'd come to be Ike Banner's right-hand man.

It was a good day to be in the hill country with a good horse under you. The range was ripe and lush with deepening summer. Mottes of shadowed timber broke the undulating slopes of meadow. Tints of azure and lavender spangled the rich carpets of grass where bluebells and larkspur poked out. Nathan spooked up occasional bunches of cattle. Long-tailed jays swooped out of the grass ahead of his horse and arched away in flirts of bright blue. A chicken hawk rode the high currents, sun flashing on its static wings.

Away to the north lay the gray shoulders of the

Palisades, whose mountainous spine provided a natural barrier for Swallowtail's top range, even if working winter-drifted cows out of the Palisade draws was a hell of a tough chore. Back there, too, was Lynchtown, a place Nathan Drew always thought of with mixed feelings.

Nathan rode steadily for an hour. He had never gone to the northwest line camp by exactly this way. But he took his own careless knowledge of the country almost for granted . . . it was that close to being an instinctive thing with him.

The sun burned along his right shoulder as he topped a bare knob and tipped his hat against sun's glare. He needed only a glance at the long tilt of wooded valley ahead of him to identify it. On its far end, which was bounded by an arm of the Palisades' foothills, was the line camp occupied by the Purleys. You couldn't make out the place from here. In fact, the valley's floor was so heavily covered with a mixed growth of spruce and cedar that hardly any open ground showed.

There were a few breaks in the trees. Nathan let his gaze touch across these in the idle way that a man did if he was used to searching for game or maybe just studying the lay of the land.

Unexpectedly, he saw something that took him so much by surprise, he wondered if he'd seen it at all. It was just a flashing glimpse, but clear enough while it lasted. A man less woods-wise might have missed it entirely. Or doubted the evidence of his own eyes.

What he had seen was a man stumbling along on foot with three other men, mounted and crowding him hard, lashing at him with what might have been ropes or whips. The four of them had cut suddenly across a slender aisle in the trees, were in plain view for an instant, and were just as suddenly swallowed by the woods again.

After his initial flick of disbelief, Nathan thought: *I saw it.* Settling the fact to his own mind that quickly and flatly.

He raised in his stirrups to stare across the blank spires of timber below. He saw no more, not even a hint of movement. A soft wind coasting up from the valley carried no whisper of sound. But what he'd witnessed must have been several hundred yards away. And it would take him a while to get there.

Nathan Drew didn't even consider doing anything else. He was Ike Banner's man and this was Ike's range. Even a man given to solitary ways and to minding his own business needn't think twice about what to do.

Heeling his mount down the slope, Nathan swerved recklessly through a field of shallow boulders that littered it. He slipped into the trees that lined the valley flats and pushed on as fast and hard as he dared. The forest was dense, but its floor was nearly free of undergrowth. The patterns of sun and shade flowing over and around him were something that would have pleasured Nathan any time he hadn't been in a violent hurry.

When he did come on the grisly tableau, it was so suddenly that he was barely able to pull up before he charged into the middle of it.

There was a good-sized clearing in the trees, and the four men were just about dead center in it. The one who was being whipped had fallen down, but one of the men on horseback had flipped a lariat over him. Now, reining sideways, he dragged his victim over the bumpy earth till the man stumbled back to his feet.

Covered with blood and dirt, he was hardly able to stand up.

The horseman gave a crazy high laugh. It was a bit like the screech of a lunatic. But then Sheb Purley wasn't altogether right in the head. Nathan had realized as much the first time he'd ever set eyes on Sheb.

The man, or rather boy, that Sheb had dragged was an Indian. His face was twisted with pain and streaming blood, and for a moment Nathan didn't recognize him. When he did, rage hit him with a pure shock. The Indian was a young cousin of his, Jimmy Hosteen.

Wild with pain and panic, Jimmy tore at the noose around his waist. But Sheb Purley, giggling with a dry monotony, kept sidling his cowpony against the dallied rope, keeping the boy off balance and stumbling.

"Just hold 'im right like that, little brother—"

Claud Purley pushed his horse forward, a doubled rope in his fist. He was getting as much fun out of the business as Sheb, but Claud wasn't crazy and he wasn't dimwitted. Claud was just pure-quill mean.

He brought the rope whistling around in a savage cut that took Jimmy Hosteen across the face. Blood spurted. The youth screamed and fell to his knees, clutching at his eyes.

Off a little to one side, the Purleys' father was sitting his horse and scratching his mouse-gray beard. He wore a mild little smile that was sort of benign because it was the only way he ever smiled.

Snake Purley. If he had any other first name, nobody ever seemed to use it. Anyway, Snake was proud of that handle, and it fit him as close as a lady's glove stretched over a charwoman's paw. He was lean and gliding, with a kind of coiled malevolence about him. He was also as smart as mustard, which you couldn't say for either of his boys.

All the same, Claud and Sheb came honestly by their Purley looks. Their sly, tough, bleach-eyed faces and hanks of strawlike hair were younger copies of their pa's. Like Snake himself, Sheb was skinny and wiry, and close to being runty. Claud, in his late twenties and maybe five years his brother's elder, had both height and heft.

He'd put a good wallop of that beef into his slashing stroke at the Hosteen boy. And was pulling his arm back for another blow when Snake drawled, "Now hold on, just hold on there a mite, boy. . . ."

Snake's quick glance had pounced on Nathan right away. But Claud hadn't noticed. With a feral glee lighting his face, he took another savage cut at Jimmy Hosteen.

Snake himself was fiddling with a long, wicked-looking whip that had a shot-loaded tip, and that tip was bright with blood. Usually he wore the whip coiled up and hung around his neck. Suddenly now, he raised it and gave it a loud crack.

"Goddammit, boy, I told you *quit!*"

Claud's pale eyes blinked in his sweating, fleshy face. He saw Nathan now. So did Sheb.

"Glory to goodness," Snake sang out mildly. "It is Mr. Nathan Drew. Have you come away over here a-seeking for us, Mr. Drew?"

Nathan rubbed a hand slowly along his thigh. He wasn't packing a gun. He didn't own a pistol; his old rifle was out of commission, being split down the stock. Otherwise he wouldn't be just sitting his horse at clearing's edge, not doing a thing.

At the moment, nothing was about all he could do.

The three Purleys watched him with those strange, hooded eyes of theirs. Waiting on his move and not troubling to hide the chill arrogance that even a raggedy trio of trash like them could summon up against a man with Indian blood.

The lower a white man was, the fiercer the pride he took in his dirty white skin, Nathan had learned. The Purleys had drifted into this country maybe a year ago, and nobody knew anything about them except the obvious. They were off-scourings of an older frontier that had its vague setting in the Ozarks. Inbred looks and a sometime-use of Old English speech stamped their kind, and why Thorp had taken them onto the crew was God's own mystery. Thorp Banner had his shortcomings, but stupidity wasn't ordinarily one of them.

The edge of Nathan's wrath bent against the cold realities of the situation. Both Snake and Claud were packing guns. Nathan lifted a hand and pointed at Jimmy Hosteen, groaning on the ground with his hands pressed over his eyes.

"That is quite a thing." Fighting to keep his voice from shaking. "Maybe you better tell me about it."

Snake tipped his head sidelong, sly and watchful. "Well then, Mr. Drew. You git sent to look in on us?"

"You might say that."

"By Mr. Thorp Banner?"

"His pa. Man who owns this whole outfit."

Snake gave a spare, reflective nod. He spat across his arm. "Glory to goodness. All right then. Little while back we come on this red nigger here butchering out one of y'r Swallowtail yearlings. We figured that a touch of the old what-for was justified."

"You did." Nathan felt his temper start to quiver on a hot rising edge once more. "I'll tell you what else you do. You get down off that horse, Mr. Purley, and you take that noose off this boy. Then you and yours hightail it the hell away from here."

Snake smiled benignly. "Ain't that a caution, now. I tell *you* what, Mr. Nathan Drew. It was Mr. Thorp Banner hired us on. It is him we takes our orders from. We are not required to take lip from no breeds."

"No?" Nathan said softly.

"That is as sure as the sun shines. Mr. Thorp Banner give us orders to keep this range clean of varmints." Snake coiled the whip in his hands. "That we aim to do. We figure this is to include cow rustlers and red niggers."

The words had barely left him when Nathan dropped lightly to the ground. He walked over to Jimmy Hosteen. The Navajo dagger flashed in his palm as he bent. One slash parted Sheb's rope. That quickly, the Indian boy was freed of it.

Sheb let out a wail of protest. "Why goddamn! Pappy, look what that son of a bitch done! My bran'-new rope . . ."

With a half-squeal half-grunt like a stuck pig's, Sheb Purley viciously reined his horse around at Nathan, whirling the slashed rope end at his head.

Nathan ducked, falling into a crouch. He came out of it almost in the same instant, the spring-steel muscles of his legs unbunching and launching him in a cat-quick leap. His body slammed against the flank of Sheb's horse; his left hand shot up to clamp around Sheb's head. Dropping back, Nathan's weight dragged Sheb out of the saddle and free of his stirrups as the panicked horse shied away.

Sheb would have tumbled to the ground except for Nathan's arm cocked around his neck, holding him upright. Grimacing against the rank unwashed smell of the youngest Purley, Nathan yanked his chin back; the Navajo blade flew up to flatten against Sheb's Adam's apple.

All of it happened very fast. One tip of the blade and Sheb would suddenly acquire an extra mouth in his throat.

Nathan didn't have to say it. The father and brother saw it; caution veiled their bleach-eyed looks.

"Breed," Snake said gently, "that will not git

you aught. You had best lay loose of him and that 'thout delay."

"As soon as you pull your guns and drop them to the ground. Then he gets loose."

"Glory to goodness. No." Snake's murmur was sibilant and stern. "That will not do at all. No sir—"

Sheb got out "Pa!" in a strangled yelp.

"No sir. You shush now, boy. There is no red nigger will bring a Purley to taw while I have the say. Claud, do you get around to the hindmost of them and I will stay front."

Nathan said flatly, "Don't. You are taking a damn long chance."

"I do not think so. I read your sign, breed. You are not about to cut my boy's throat." Snake motioned sharply at his older son. "Goddammit, make haste there!"

Claud grinned. Taking just enough time about it to show how independent he was, he edged his horse in a wide circle around back of Nathan. Snake stayed where he was, and now both of them negligently eased the pistols out of their homemade rawhide holsters.

"There now, breed," said Snake. "Lay loose of him. Or honest to Jesus, we will blow you to glory from two ways, and no mistake."

Nathan thought the degenerate bastards might do just that, even if it cost Sheb his life. But if he did let go of Sheb, would it make any difference?

Snake was blandly smart enough to run a good bluff, but given the streak of wild instability in this crew, you couldn't assume anything for sure.

Something made a whirring hiss. There was a *thunk* of stone hitting wood.

The Purleys exchanged startled looks. But Nathan Drew was the first to see what had made the peculiar sound. Just behind Snake and to his left, an arrow quivered in a cedar trunk. Part of its black obsidian head protruded.

"That's a Navajo arrow in the tree back of you," he said quietly. "Have a look."

Snake twisted in his saddle, staring. Claud whirled his horse in a panic, pistol up and cocked as he peered wildly into the trees. "Jesus, Pappy—!"

"You're looking the wrong way," Nathan murmured. "He's on your left and a little to your rear. And I wouldn't bring that gun to bear if I were you. He has a couple friends along."

Claud looked and gaped. An Indian was standing by a big spruce tree maybe five yards away. The neutral colors of his clout and leggings and headband were almost invisible in the dappling of sun and shadow. But silver and turquoise winked on the heavy leather bow guard that protected his left wrist. An arrow lay nocked on his drawn bow, and it was leveled straight at Claud.

Nathan added to Snake, "The other two are square in back of you, Mr. Purley. I'd go easy."

Snake had been squinting at the Navajo bowman, swearing softly and fingering his pistol. Now he stiffened and turned in his saddle once more, but very slowly this time. Two Indians stood under the trees. They wore trousers and calico shirts and carried rifles. These were up and pointed at the Purleys.

"*Taadoo naki nani*!" Nathan raised his voice, speaking loudly in Navajo.

Snake's bleach eyes narrowed. "What's at? You be keerful, breed. I can still send you to glory faster'n you can bat a winker."

"I told them they can see Jimmy Hosteen is alive . . . to hold their fire and I will send you away." Nathan let go of Sheb and gave him a push toward his horse. "I'd put those guns away, Mr. Purley, and then I'd get some distance between me and these fellows. You make a wrong move, any move at all but to put your iron away and pack out of here, and you'll be dead men. All three of you."

He said it very softly and positively.

Snake swore once and jammed his gun into its holster. He coiled his whip, lifted off his hat, dropped the whip over his neck and replaced the hat. Gathering his reins, he said to Sheb, "Get into saddle. Leather that hogleg, Claud."

"One thing," said Nathan. "Where is that cow you say he butchered?"

Snake worked his mouth and spat thinly.

"Indin, you find it y'self. Goddammit, Sheb, get up there—"

Sheb stood by his mount, leaning one hand on the saddle leather. The other hand was fisted so tight, the knuckles were white. So was his face under its dirty beard stubble. He was fixing Nathan with a stare that held a baleful distillation of crazy-eyed hate.

Claud reined over by him, muttering, "Come on, ol' Loonie-as-a-Bedbug. Get 'long now!" And gave his brother a hard cuff on the ear.

Sheb moved like a sleepwalker. But he moved, hitching himself into stirrup and swinging astride his nag. He never took his eyes off Nathan.

Bunched together, the Purleys rode out of the clearing. They did it with a contemptuous lack of haste, and the Indians' weapons stayed trained on them till the trees swallowed them.

Some of the tension slid from Nathan's muscles. For a moment there, the situation had seemed to hang on a hair's-breadth. Looking at Jimmy Hosteen on the ground, he had a grim foretaste that it wasn't over with yet. Killing could still come out of this.

Nathan dropped on one knee beside the boy.

Jimmy was twitching and shuddering in the convulsions of raw pain, moaning and half-conscious. The sight of him was enough to turn a strong man's stomach. His shirt and pants were full of bloody tears. He must have been lashed and driven mercilessly for a good ways even before Nathan had first spotted him. Snake had gotten in plenty of licks with that shot-tipped whip of his. Across the boy's back and chest and arms, dime-sized bits of skin had been lifted off as neatly as a knife could have done. Those patches were streaming blood.

Nathan's flesh crawled. He reached for the boy's arms to pull his hands away from his face.

"Don't touch him, *Belinkana*," a voice said in Navajo.

Nathan Drew looked up.

The bowman stood above him, legs spraddled. Lean and nervous and burning-eyed, he, like Nathan, was a blood relation of the hurt boy. So were the other two Indians, who had moved forward to gaze wordlessly down at Jimmy Hosteen. They were twins named Sam and George Hosteen, stolid men in their thirties. The bowman, too, bore the family name of Hosteen, but he hated it. He was ready to fight to the death a man who addressed him by anything but his Navajo name.

Nathan rocked back on his heels. "Suit yourself, Adakhai," he said in English, mildly. "But someone better look at him. I would hazard he may have lost an eye. Maybe both eyes."

Adakhai dropped to his haunches, caught hold of Jimmy Hosteen's wrists and pried his hands away from his face. One eye was squinted shut in a welter of blood. The other eye hung partly out of its socket, a jellied carnage.

Adakhai let out a long hissing sound. "For this thing, there will be . . . you white-eyes have a saying. An eye for an eye."

Nathan said coldly, flatly, "No. It won't be that way."

"Do you say so, *Belinkana*?"

"I say it. So will Jack Lynch, the father of your mother."

"Jack Lynch doesn't give me orders. He is a white-eyes like you."

"You call me an 'American' or a 'white-eyes' again," Nathan said thinly, "you might get that fight you're spoiling for so damn bad. And you won't have to look for it any farther than right smack where you're squatting."

Oddly, Adakhai smiled. It was a smile thin with contempt, but bitterly amused all the same. "What do you call yourself, Drew? You are a bat, maybe. Not a mouse and not a bird."

"Jimmy has some white blood. So do Sam and George here. You have a splash of it yourself."

Adakhai's narrow face turned wolfish. "We don't live with the *Belinkana*!" he spat. "We don't clean manure out of their stables. I would die before I shoveled shit for a white-eyes!"

Nathan came to his feet, and Adakhai swiftly matched his movement, saying hotly, "*Chindash*! Get away from here, *Belinkana*! We will look to our own."

CHAPTER 2

It wasn't often that Ike Banner called a family conference. When he did, it was generally to lay down the law about one thing or another to his sons. None of these caucuses could be described as friendly discussions, and like as not they would bring out a blaze of Ike's crusty temper. Mellowed by age or not, he still had one.

After Nathan Drew reported to him on the clash between the Purley clan and the Lynchtown Navajos, Ike had sent Mexican house servants to summon his three sons. While he and Nathan waited for them in the big front parlor of Swallowtail's main house, Ike stomped up and down the parlor floor, quietly cursing, ignoring the twinges of pain that convulsed his arthritis-wracked body.

At seventy, he was still immensely wide of shoulder and girthed like a hogshead. Not a pound of it was fat, in spite of the rheumatic agony that had confined a lot of his activity over the last few years. Ike's bushing plume of hair and heavy mustaches had only recently turned snow-white. His face had been as tan and seamed as a walnut for as far back as Nathan remembered. Sawed-off and stocky, he'd been half a head shorter than Aunt Lu. Many had sniggered about that, but never in Ike Banner's presence.

Halting by the blackened fieldstone fireplace, hands shoved in his hip pockets, he wheeled toward Nathan, wincing with the abruptness of his movement. "Nate, just how bad you reckon that Hosteen boy was damaged?"

Nathan, slacked in a rawhide-rigged armchair, lifted one shoulder. "Well, he has lost an eye for sure. Outside of that, he was only cut up, but bad enough. That's not so much the point."

"I know, I know." Ike started pacing again; he scrubbed a hand over his jaw. "Indian can take a lot of pain for granted. It's the face he loses to an enemy. Nate—"

"Yes."

"Tomorrow you and me will ride to Lynchtown. Talk to Jack Lynch."

"Think you can manage that far a ride?"

"Goddammit, yes!"

Nathan shrugged faintly.

He tipped his gaze away from the older man, letting it wander over the room, familiar and full of good memories. This biggest of the two parlors was Ike's domain, large and high-ceilinged, comfortable with shabby furnishings of old leather chairs and settees. The walls were hung with trophy heads of grizzly and bighorn, a collection of antique flintlocks and cutlasses, and several colorful *bayeta* blankets of Navajo make. Yet the few touches that Aunt Lu had contributed to this masculine den, incongruous Doré prints and a couple of fancy hassocks that Ike had grumbled about having installed, still remained in place.

That simple fact said a lot about the kind of life one man and one woman had known together.

Then why had the rest of the Banner household gone so sadly awry? No way of answering for sure, Nathan mused. Like didn't always beget like, and the best of blood went sour. Just as often you'd find a pair of reprobates hatching out a solid citizen, and no explaining that either.

These were old thoughts, and he was considering them phlegmatically when Ike broke silence again. "That one Hosteen cousin, what's his name, the hothead."

"Adakhai."

"If there's trouble in the budding, he'll make it. You think so?"

"He will start it off," said Nathan. "There's others in Lynchtown will follow his lead."

"Yeah. I was afraid of that." Ike rubbed his forehead as if it ached intolerably. "I hope to Christ old Jack can . . ."

He broke off as boots came clumping onto the porch. The front door pushed open and Thorp Banner came tramping in like a rank gust. On his heels was Freeman, his youngest brother. Both had just returned from a day's work on-range.

"What's up, Pa?" Thorp's eyes were as bright as blue marbles; they shifted to Nathan. Thorp grinned and nodded.

If Ike hadn't been present, Nathan knew, Thorp would have greeted him with a cheery, "How there, chief! Thought I smeltum beargrease," or maybe, "Hey, look who's hunkered in our wigwam." He was pretty well stocked with witticisms of that sort.

Thorp Banner was a large, rawboned man who towered above his father and brothers. In that, Ike always said, he took after Luella's pa ("Hell's bells, but that was a big man!"). Ordinarily, there might have been some griping from the crew when a man elevated his own son to the foremanship of one of the territory's biggest ranches. Not a man in the outfit had questioned Thorp's right to the position in these five years. Just a look of his ice-chill eyes was enough to quell the notion.

And Thorp was a damned good foreman. Nobody could deny that. He worked his butt off for Swallowtail from dawn till quitting time and still gave off, at the end of a working day, a feel of crackling, suppressed energy.

"Hello," Ike said gruffly. "You wasn't raised in any sty that I know of, so take off your hats. Sit down."

Thorp did, swiping his dusty Stetson against his chaps and tossing it in a vacant chair. He walked over to a settee opposite Nathan and dropped into it, scooping a boyish lick of sandy, prematurely graying hair off his brow. It topped a long, jut-jawed face scoured by sun and wind to a deep mahogany. His splay-fingered hand showed the man's brute power. Most men who worked cattle were careful of their hands, a consideration that never bothered Thorp. His hands were paws: hairy and hamlike, broken more than once in work or play, crosshatched with twisty white scars.

Freeman didn't yank his hat off till Thorp did. Afterward he sailed it into the same vacant chair and slacked bonelessly onto the settee alongside Thorp.

Free, twelve years younger than Thorp's thirty-three, was like a smaller, unformed version of his big brother, whom he worshipped, naturally. Free had a streak of reckless cruelty in him, and not much of Thorp's calculating nature to hold it in check. It showed in his treatment of horses, and—so gossip had it—in his treatment of bordello girls.

"Well, what is it, Pa?" Thorp asked. "You want to chew out our what-fors about something? Or just what is it?"

"Soon as Ty joins us. You'll hear it then."

Free snickered. "Pa, you waiting on old Tyrone any time after noon, you could wait till tomorrow. By this time he has climbed into his bottle and pulled the cork in after him."

Thorp slapped him on the knee and let out a hearty bray of laughter.

Ike gave a sour grunt. "All right, Nate. Tell 'em."

Nathan told of his adventure with the Purleys. His thoughts were more on Thorp's reactions than on his own words. Not that Thorp revealed anything more than an idle interest. He listened impassively, now and then swiping a thumb across his jaw.

Another thing Ike had said that Thorp got from his maternal grandfather was his loud, boisterous ways. What Nathan had noticed most was that his boisterousness tended to conceal a quick, clever side of Thorp that never missed a thing. Anytime something was going on in his vicinity, he was always in the forefront of the action. The funny thing about Thorp was that for all his roaring appetites, nothing ever touched him in a feeling way. A piece of his mind stayed cool and appraising through anything that happened to him. Whether that was for good or bad, Nathan didn't know.

One thing he was sure of was that underneath it all, Thorp Banner was the most cold-blooded son of a bitch he had ever met. Not many people glimpsed that side of Thorp. Ike, for all his shrewdness in dealing with men, had a blind spot about his eldest son.

When Nathan paused after telling of how the Purleys had withdrawn when the three Navajos had arrived on the scene, Thorp leaned forward, set his elbows on his knees and laced his big paws loosely together.

"All right now," he said. "What about that Swallowtail beef they said this Injun kid killed and butchered? That's what interests me."

"I'm coming to that."

Nathan said that before parting from the Navajos, he had asked the Hosteen twins, Sam and George, what had brought them on the scene so providentially. Not as hostile as Adakhai, the brothers had told Nathan that they and Adakhai and Jimmy Hosteen had gone out together for a day's hunting, and had decided to split up. They were supposed to rendezvous at noon, and when Jimmy hadn't shown up at the agreed-on site, they had gone looking for him.

Knowing the general area in which he was hunting, they had covered it quickly enough. They had found a dead cow that wore a Swallowtail brand, and it was partly butchered, all right. Jimmy had skinned it out and had started to quarter it with his hand ax. That sign was plain to read, and so was the fact that he had been surprised by three horsemen. After that, they had quickly followed up Jimmy Hosteen and his tormentors.

Nathan himself had gone to the spot to check out the story. The butchered steer was where the brothers had told him it was, and it was branded Swallowtail.

"Well, there you are." Thorp spread his paws. "What's all the fuss about? The kid took a cow of ours. Men have got hung for less."

"But not whipped to raw meat first," Nathan said tonelessly. "They would have done him to death if I hadn't shown up."

Thorp snorted gently. "Boy, that's easy to guess on."

"There's more. After I checked on that butchered cow, I cut back to head off the Hosteens. They had rigged a travois to put Jimmy on and were on their way back to Lynchtown. I hoped Jimmy might be conscious by then . . . that he could maybe tell me his side of it. He was awake. Enough to tell me he had mistaken that Swallowtail cow for a deer."

Thorp gave a chuckle and a shake of his head, murmuring, "Oh Jesus."

Ike snapped, "Just hold your horses before you hand down any verdicts. Nate, what do you think?"

"Could have happened that way. That cow was downed in heavy woods. Easy for a man's eyes to play tricks on him in the woods. It's happened a lot. Even to Indians."

"If it was an accident," said Thorp, "why in hell did he butcher the critter out?"

"Said he couldn't just leave it lay. He knew if a shot cow turned up, you'd blame the whole Lynchtown crowd. It would make trouble they don't need. So he figured to cut up the carcass and pack it out."

"Bullshit," Thorp said flatly.

Ike halted in his slow pacing and glared at his son. "Goddammit, that's enough. You're passing judgment where you can't be sure."

Thorp clapped his hands on his knees. "I'm *damn* well sure. I always said those Lynchtown bastards been robbing us blind. Killing a few of our beeves at a time and hustling the meat away. Hell, you've seen our range tallies. Why does that north part show a heavy loss every spring?"

"Winterkill. Cattle try to winter in those foothill passes and get drifted in. Hell, we been over all this before."

"Ah shit, winterkill. What it is, our beef has been winding up in them Navajos' stewpots for better'n twenty years."

Ike combed a hand through his thick hair, scowling. "You've spent a deal of time at Lynchtown, Nate. You eaten their grub often enough. What do you say?"

Nathan shrugged. "Mutton or venison is what they always served me. If there was any beef around, I never tasted it." Looking at Thorp, he added, "Only being a half-breed and kin of theirs, it's more than likely I have covered up for them all these years."

Thorp grinned. "Well, sir, you're the one just said it, ain't you?"

"Quit that," Ike said testily. "Thorp, more and more I have tried to put the running of Swallowtail in your hands. Won't be long before the whole shebang is yours anyway. But you taken a wrong tack with those Lynchtown people right along. You best get on their right side or you'll cook up a whole kettle of trouble for yourself one day."

"I'll say it again, Pa. Bullshit. That gang of siwashes is squatting on our land. *Ours,* by God, patented to us free and clear."

"That's 'cause I coddle 'em. You might's well say it. You always do."

"If you are asking for plain talk, I'll give you some. You have let those Lynchtown breeds piss all over us. Squatting on our land, high-grading our beef, running their goats and woolies all over our good range and spoiling it for cattle. All because you and Jack Lynch was trapping partners way-to-God back when."

Ike nodded impassively. "That cuts no ice with you."

"Not a sliver." Thorp made a fist, pointed the index finger out and shook it at his father. "I'll tell you something else flat out. I am good and damn sick of it. When the time comes, I mean to wipe our range clean of that goddamn pesthole . . . Lynchtown."

"When I pass over, you mean."

"Well—"

"Don't gamble on that, boy." Ike's tone went very quiet. "Even when I have passed over, don't lay odds on it."

"What the hell is that supposed to mean?"

Ike was angry, Nathan could see. Angry enough to speak out as bluntly as Thorp had. But the moment was broken as Ty Banner and his wife entered the room.

Ty limped in from a corridor that led to the back of the low, rambling house. He was braced by a crutch on one side, and on the other side by Serena. Ty had walked with a crutch since his accident several years ago, but when he also needed to lean on someone, it meant he'd drunk too much. Lately, it wasn't unusual for him to get so pie-eyed by noon that he'd have to spend the afternoon in bed.

Serena helped Ty ease himself into a chair. He sent a puffy-eyed look around the room, yawning. "Well, Pa. I trust you have an adequately urgent reason for calling recess on a man's beauty sleep."

Free snickered. Thorp slapped his knee and laughed. Ty himself showed the edge of a weary grin. But all three of them sobered under the chill blaze of Ike's blue eyes. The old man's temper was up, and no mistake.

Having seated Ty, his wife retreated toward the hallway. "You stay, girl," Ike said gruffly. "You're family too."

Obediently, Serena walked to a hassock and sat, folding her hands in her lap. She was a blond, slender girl whose best feature was her fine gray eyes. She had a delicate, pale beauty too, but it had always seemed kind of washed-out to Nathan. He felt sorry for Serena. Aunt Lu had never been cowed by this household of men; her spirit had been like gentle iron. Serena, on the other hand, was so quietly and desperately timid that life would be an ordeal for her even if she hadn't wed Tyrone Banner.

Thorp grinned at her. "Say, there. You looking as fine as frog-hair today, sister-in-law."

Serena turned her gaze downward, blushing. Thorp whooped with delight. "Look at that! Why, the way ol' See pinks up, you wouldn't think she was a three-year's-wed lady ay-tall."

Ty's drowsy look had vanished. He watched Thorp narrowly. Not saying anything, just watching him.

"Who you looking so sandy at all at once, Sleepy?" Thorp asked amiably.

"You," Ty said thinly. "I suggest you get in the habit of choosing your words, brother mine."

"Well, boy howdy! All I said—"

"I heard what you said."

"Stop that damn wrangling!" Ike roared. "I got more to say, and you'll all pipe down and hear me out! And Thorp—you put a curb on that tongue of yours." He paused, bridling the surge

44

of his wrath. "Nate, tell it once more for these two, will you?"

For the third time, Nathan told of his encounter with the Purleys.

Ty listened without much interest, blinking a little owlishly. He had a keener mind than any of them, but lately he'd rarely honed it to any sort of problem. Once he had also been the handsomest Banner, as fair and blond as his wife. Now, at twenty-six, he was already edging toward a middle-aged grossness that was slightly repulsive. Ty's stocky body had gone soft and heavy; his face was florid, its fine-boned features lost in a sheath of unhealthy flesh.

When Nathan had finished, Ike said, "I am trying to get a vote here, Tyrone. What you think we should do about this?"

Ty gave a meager shrug. "I'd like to hear what Nate says."

Thorp pushed his lips out sardonically. "That don't call for no wild guess."

"Shut your mouth for a little while, all right?" Ike glanced at Nathan. "Well, Nate?"

Nathan said unhesitatingly, "I'd get rid of those Purleys. They're trash and they're trouble. Keep them on and you will likely get more of the same."

"Pull 'em off that line-camp duty, you mean?"

"Partly. That line camp is too close to Lynchtown. After what they did to Jimmy

Hosteen, some of the young men may be hell-for-leather to collect Purley scalps. Then Swallowtail will have a little war on its hands." Nathan paused, locking eyes with Thorp. "What else I'd do, I'd fire those Purleys outright. Get them off Swallowtail."

"I take it," Thorp said gently, "you are questioning my judgment in hiring those fellows."

"Well, sir, you're the one just said it." Nathan's face was unreadable as he turned Thorp's words back on him.

It scored. Thorp showed a frosty grin. "I got no complaints about how they do their job. Those boys are hard workers. And if they turn up any cattle-killing siwashes they want to bust wide open, it's fine with me."

"All right."

"What do you mean, 'all right'?" Thorp's grin widened, exposing his big teeth. "Nate, you better get straight who is running this shebang—"

"That's still me," Ike cut in harshly. "And don't you forget it. Thorp, you listen—"

"No. You hear me now, Pa. All of you hear me. Now I assigned old Snake and his boys to that line camp a-purpose. I know damn well those Navajos from Lynchtown been stealing our beef. I told the Purleys to watch out for 'em and to deal as they seen fit with any they caught redhanded." Thorp arced a thumb against his chest. "What they done today, they done under my orders. Either I give the orders in this outfit, or I don't. Either I hire and fire like I want, or I don't. Either I'm foreman of Swallowtail, or I ain't. Now. Which is it?"

His stare challenged his father.

After a long cold moment, Ike said quietly, "Put it like that, I guess you ain't."

"Pa?" Thorp sounded disbelieving.

"I mean that. Thorp, you got a lot to learn about people. Dealing with people. Maybe you'll learn, maybe not. Meantime, don't forget who's still the big augur of this outfit. Long as I got life in me, that's me."

Thorp's stare turned livid; a vein squirmed in his temple. But he said nothing.

"There's a choice," Ike told him. "Tomorrow you ride out to that line camp and give them Purleys their time, or I'll look for a new ramrod."

"Maybe"—Thorp's lips barely stirred—"you ought to get yourself a half-breed foreman."

"No more of your lip. What is it? Yes or no?"

Thorp's head dipped as he got abruptly to his feet. "I'm just a lousy foreman. I take orders from the owner."

"That's yes?"

"Yes, goddammit. Yes."

Thorp scooped up his hat, gave it a savage bat against his thigh, and started for the door. Ike's voice halted him.

"You mind, now. I ain't just giving notice. I want the Purleys off Swallowtail by sundown tomorrow."

"Sure," Thorp said softly. He raised his arm with the Stetson in his fist, pointing it at Nathan. "Talk about trouble, Pa. You know what the real trouble is? You listen to that breed ahead of me. You take his word above mine all the damned time."

"That ain't true—" Ike began sharply. But Thorp had already gone out the door, slamming it behind him.

CHAPTER 3

After Thorp's exit, there wasn't much point in continuing the discussion. Free ambled out, and shortly afterward Nathan Drew excused himself. Ike returned to his office in an adjoining room.

Ty was starting to doze off in his chair. Serena laid a hand on his shoulder and gently shook him. "Dear," she said.

"Huh?"

"Hadn't you better go back to bed if you're going to nap some more?"

"Oh, yeah. I guess so."

He climbed leadenly to his feet, braced by his crutch, and clamped an arm around Serena's shoulders. Together they swayed down the corridor to their back bedroom. Ty collapsed across the bed, almost pulling her down with him. Serena straightened up, but he took hold of her wrist.

"Come here," he said thickly.

"No, Ty. Please. I have to give the cook orders for supper . . ."

"Come here, See darling. Come down here."

"Ty, please—"

"Damn it, See! Come here, I said."

He dragged her close, his free hand fumbling with the neck of her dress. She quit straining away from him, passive in his grasp as he started to unbutton her dress. His hand slipped inside, pushing into her chemise, cupping the soft rondure of a breast.

Then the hand withdrew. "Serena . . ."

Her eyes were tightly closed. Serena opened them, seeing his reddened, puffy eyes blinking at her, full of remorse. "Oh God. I'm sorry, See."

"Then please, will you let go of me?"

He released her wrist and she turned away, buttoning up her dress.

"What a bastard I am. God, See."

Serena turned slowly back to him, her underlip trembling. She pressed her teeth into it. A warm knot tightened in her throat and she felt like crying. Sitting on the edge of the bed, she took his hand in hers.

"It's all right, dear. Do try to get a little more sleep. You'll feel better when you've had something to eat."

Ty grimaced faintly. He shut his eyes and lay quietly, his hand loose in hers.

Tearlessly, Serena let her gaze trace the bloated lines of his face, trying to erase them in her mind's eye. It was getting harder and harder to remember the handsome and elegant Tyrone Banner of a few years ago.

Ty had never possessed what you'd call a sunny disposition. And certainly not an even one. Like many artistic types, his moods were jack-in-the-box: buoyant at one time, blackly brooding another time. The peaks and plunges of his temperament hadn't greatly troubled Serena when she'd first known him. They were part of Ty, after all, and she'd loved Ty. And still did. Seemingly, the fact would never change. But in the last year, it had drawn her into a kind of despair.

At times, loving him or not, she hardly thought she could stand their life together any longer.

What could you do but despair of a man who was gifted with a fine mind and an outstanding talent and was letting them wither uselessly away? For the fates that had formed Ty Banner had left some vital iron out of his being. He was one of those too-sensitive souls who stood up badly to the ordinary maulings of life.

Serena had believed she could give him a needed infusion of strength by her love. She knew better now. It was a bitter reality that she lived with day by day. What strength did she have to give anyone? High-strung, nervous, withdrawn, she had acted courageously just once in her life. That was when she had defied her domineering father in order to marry Ty Banner.

When this had proved to be exactly as much of a mistake as her father had predicted, Serena's self-esteem had plunged still lower. Maybe, she thought drearily, that was all a pair of weaklings such as Ty and she could do for each other: hang onto one another while they sank together.

Yet in spite of their built-in flaws, things might so easily have gone differently for them! *If.* So many things, so many vagaries of blind chance, happened over which people had no control. . . .

Ty had always been different, even as a child. "All the time reading or drawing pictures," his father had told her. "I never seen the beat." Ike had also admitted that he'd tried his damnedest to break Ty out of these habits, to shape him toward a man's world, the rough world of a working ranch. It had been a mistake, Ike now admitted, "Like teaching a fish to swim out o' water."

It had driven the boy deeper into himself, back to the apron strings of a perplexed mother who hardly understood him any better. And in his late teens, finally, it had sparked rebellion. At that point, a disgusted Ike had consented to send Ty away to San Francisco, where he could live with a married sister of Luella's and attend an art academy.

In a period of four years, Ty had made a happy adjustment to the excitements of a bustling city that boasted currents of Spanish and American and Chinese cultures, political and social turbulence, thriving artists' enclaves, the best of theater and opera. He had loved it all. And had spilled out his enthusiasm to Serena on the evening they met, at a gala social affair for young people in her uncle's Nob Hill mansion.

Serena's staid parents had whipped her young life into a predictable mold. One that, as an obedient and timid-natured daughter, she had never questioned. Tyrone Banner, young and vibrant and handsome, glowing with the fervor of an artistic visionary, had completely enthralled her. Opened her eyes to all that life might be—she had thought at the time.

The two of them had met often. Sometimes openly on social occasions; at other times secretly: alone together, as it were. Both had been caught up in a mad, total whirl of infatuation. If not for that, Serena supposed, she'd never have mustered the courage—after Ty had asked her father's consent and was curtly refused—to elope with him.

Ty had been afire with plans. He would, he had averred against Serena's dismayed objections, abandon his dream of becoming an artist of the highest creative caliber. It would, after all, mean more years of study and work and (as he'd put it) "a lot of kiss-ass posturing" for which he had no taste, in order to get showings of his work at major galleries. What would they live on, mean-time? As a married man he had responsibilities to shoulder, a wife he was determined to support in decent style.

What they would do for a honeymoon trip was

travel to his family's ranch in New Mexico. There, Ty had sternly resolved, he would apply himself to learning the ranching business. Even in his youthful indifference, he had absorbed a good deal of know-how about Swallowtail's workings; he'd pick up plenty more once he started applying himself. And would do Serena and his family and himself proud. ("You wait and see, honey. I really will.")

Ty was snoring gently now, his mouth partly open.

Serena gazed down at his hand that lay lax in hers. A slender and long-fingered, yet strong hand which—she remembered one of Ty's instructors at the San Francisco Academy of Art telling her—contained intricacies of nerve and muscle that, backed by his superb talent, could make of him another Rembrandt, whose dark-warm tones he favored—or even a Botticelli, in whose style of classic humanism he was already starting to excel.

Could have made.

Suddenly, again, Serena felt like weeping. Oh God. What fools they had been. Both of them.

Despite her own instinctive misgivings, she hadn't been able to spell out a valid reason for them to Ty. Even if she'd been able to, it might have made little difference. Her new husband had taken a bit in his teeth and was determined to run with it. His considerable intellect couldn't offset a streak of perverse impracticality that came of being a born romantic.

So they had gone to Swallowtail. For a time, everything had seemed to turn up rosy. Ty's father and mother had welcomed the newlyweds with open arms. Ike was impressed by the change in his second son. Luella, on the other hand, had been vaguely troubled. She'd confided as much to Serena, who shared her feeling. Serena had found a friend and confidant in her mother-in-law, but there'd been little time to realize whatever advantages of advice or support Luella might have given. Within a few weeks of Ty's return to Swallowtail, his mother had suddenly died of a stroke.

For some months Ty had plunged into his new career with a will. He had spent whole days on-range in all kinds of weather, and had worked as hard as any puncher. He had spent hours with his father, going over the ranch books, asking questions, learning the whole business end.

But inside of a year he was getting bored and restless. It had been inevitable, Serena saw now. Ty was a born artist, first and last. He needed a challenge that was abstract and creative, not concrete and physical.

He had known it and wouldn't admit it. For a time he'd kept fighting his own nature. Serena had felt the strain as badly as he. If not for her, Ty could have returned to his art with a clear conscience. Only his man's pride in properly supporting the woman he loved kept him plugging doggedly along at Swallowtail, while his anger grew and so did Serena's sense of guilt.

Then the drinking had begun, the frequent trips to town which might last for several days, ending in his returning hungover and chastened, ready to work again. Ike had spoken impatiently to him; his brothers had twitted him, humorously at first, then with open contempt. He'd become unbearable to be around. Serena had been at her wit's end when the accident happened.

Goaded to an insensate rage by something Thorp or Free had said derogatory to his manhood, Ty had attempted to rough-break a horse Nathan Drew was having trouble getting gentled. Having his own horse-breaking methods, Nathan had tried to talk Ty out of it. But Ty had savagely overridden all objections and had topped the mustang. He had been thrown and then trampled, both his legs shattered.

The weeks that had followed had been a nightmare. Ty had been kept almost constantly dosed with morphine, while doctors Ike had sent for examined his legs and gave grim verdicts, one after another. The left leg would heal, though crookedly and misshapenly. The right leg hadn't looked as bad, but there was nerve damage. Ty had been confined to a wheelchair for nearly a year. When he could walk again, he had needed a crutch to support him on his right side without pain. Idiotic in his pride, as always, he refused to use the two crutches that would have made getting about less of an ordeal. . . .

Serena tightly shut her eyes and then opened them. She'd done all her crying long ago. Ty continued to snore. Gently, she detached her hand from his and rose to her feet.

She had duties to attend to. Mostly they consisted of giving orders to the help, but she was no Luella Banner. After three years, she still felt ill-equipped to fill that strong woman's shoes, and she acted it. Ike was tolerant of her gaffes; all the same he expected her, as the sole female member of his family, to fill a proper place in his household.

I hate to order anyone about, she thought: *I just hate it.* But Celestina, the house cook, would be awaiting her orders for supper. And growing crosser by the moment.

Serena tiptoed to the door and stepped into the corridor, softly closing the door after her. Then she turned—and stopped in her tracks. Thorp Banner was lounging by the doorway of his room near the end of the hall.

Idly drawing on a stogie, he gave her a sly and sleepy-eyed look. " 'Lo there, See."

"Hello."

She would have to walk closely past him. Serena felt a lurch of dismay in her stomach. She was resolved not to show it. Putting on a face as calm as her name suggested, she moved briskly down the hall.

Just as she came abreast of Thorp, his hand shot out and slapped against the opposite wall. His arm was a bar across her way. Serena made herself meet his eyes.

"May I get by, please? I have to give the orders for supper."

"Honey," Thorp drawled, "you know what? I have always figured you had a talent for taking orders, not giving 'em."

His lips framed that big horsey crooked grin of his that was anything but amused. The rank smell of him, a rich stink of horse and harness and old sweat, was so heavy in Serena's nostrils that she nearly took a step backward. The only times Thorp ever cleaned up was when he took dinner with the family, which wasn't any more often than Ike insisted he do so. Thorp liked to eat with the crew and occupy the head of the cook-shack table.

"Fact is"—he shifted his weight toward her, and now she did flinch away—"I have thought it would be nice to give you an order or two, See. Yessirree. . . ."

Bravely, Serena kept her gaze steady on his. "And what is that supposed to mean?"

Thorp jerked his head back; a mild bray of laughter burst from him. With it came a sickish-sweet roll of whiskey smell that nearly gagged her.

Thorp had never made any secret of his lascivious designs on her, but at least he'd confined them to long hot stares and an occasional suggestive remark, nothing very offensive and never in the presence of others. Yet Serena had always been afraid of him. He was big and overpowering, rough as a rock and just as lacking in sentiment of any kind. But clever enough to keep his utter brutishness in rein.

The rein had slipped. A red recklessness flickered in his eyes, lust heated by liquor. His hand left the wall and swung to rest on her shoulder.

"Why," he said softly, mockingly, "come down here, See darling. Come down here. That is what I mean. Bet you could do that for a man real nice. I would admire to know. Do you?"

Ty's words to her. He had been listening. Serena felt her skin crawl. The only other thing she felt, just now, was pure terror.

Thorp said grinning, "Cat got your tongue, honey?" His fingers lightly kneaded her shoulder; he blew a plume of smoke in her face.

Serena coughed, her eyes watering. She swiped the back of her hand across them. When she could see again, Thorp's face had tipped close to hers. His great leering grin was inches away. She would have backed off, but her limbs felt paralyzed. Her throat was too dry to form words—

"Hey, brother."

Free had stepped unnoticed into the hall. He stood grinning at the scene. "How 'bout a game o' horseshoes before supper? Or you got something better in mind?"

Thorp let out a throaty bellow of mirth. "My sakes. Now what's more fun than horseshoes?" He patted Serena's shoulder and took his hand away. "You are a mighty understanding sister-in-law, you know that?"

Their spurs rang on the hardwood floor as they tramped out. Her knees weak as water, Serena leaned her back against the wall. She pressed a hand to her throat where a sick pulse throbbed. In all her young life, she had never known what fear really was.

Now she knew.

CHAPTER 4

It hadn't been easy for Nathan Drew to find his place at Swallowtail. In some ways, more than twenty years after that cold fall day when his mother had brought him here, he still didn't fit into the ordinary texture of life on the great ranch. Mostly Nathan kept to himself. He was a man caught between two worlds, not really at home in either one, and he was a natural loner. He had his place now, but it was that of a lone man, and he lived it contentedly.

Some years back, Ike Banner had gone into a marginal business: raising horses for sale to the U. S. Army. The man he'd assigned to the task was Diego Cruz, an ancient Mexican wrangler who had hunted mustangs most of his life and had an uncanny feeling for horseflesh. A demanding job, it was one old Diego couldn't hope to handle for very many years. So he'd asked Ike if he might take on young Nathan as his apprentice and general helper.

It had been a sound choice. Nathan had shared the old man's feeling for horses, and under Diego Cruz's tutelage he had grown into the job naturally and easily. The U. S. Cavalry wanted only the finest mounts. Any defects would be spotted at once by a line officer even if they got past the regimental vet, and you couldn't invest years of work in an animal and then risk a turndown.

Now that Diego was in effect retired, Nathan had taken over the whole job. Ike gave him a completely free hand; nobody stood over him, including the foreman. That was how Nathan liked it—quite aside from the fact that he'd have quit Swallowtail before he'd take an order from Thorp Banner. Nathan had his own quarters in an old log hut not far from the stables; he prepared his own meals there and tended his own business. That was his life, except for the occasional odd duty to which Ike assigned him.

Nathan also rough-broke and gentled mustangs for Swallowtail's own use, whenever that job wanted doing. Wild-horse hunters showed up now and then with wildlings they had captured, and if the outfit needed any, Nathan would take the pick of them. He drove shrewd bargains, and his choices rarely turned out badly. The mustang that had savaged and crippled Ty Banner had been one of those few. Ty had been fairly warned, of course. All the same, Nathan had often wished he'd used force, if necessary, to prevent Ty from topping that crazy bronc.

This morning Nathan was working over another refractory horse. It was a wicked job.

With the help of Sandal Cruz, old Diego's grandson, he drove the dun mustang into a tight handling chute rigged between the small holding pen and the big breaking corral. The dun was in a vicious mood; he lashed out with his hoofs at the confining chute. It took them a good fifteen minutes to put on the double-rigged saddle and braided hackamore.

Nathan climbed to the top of the chute and lowered himself into the saddle. Then he told Sandal to "let 'er rip." The youth swung open the gate. The dun went high-rolling into the corral. He plunged up and down in great pile-driving leaps that threatened to wrench Nathan's spine apart. Then he switched to sunfishing, forcing his rider to constantly shift his center of balance. Finally, he began to pioneer, changing direction at every plunge.

A man's frame could absorb only so much of such punishment. Nathan took a dive from the saddle and hit the ground in a loose horse-breaker's roll. Getting away from the driving hoofs, he scrambled out through the corral poles.

Old Diego Cruz, a wiry gnome of a man with a puckered-leather face, stood looking on. His shoulders jerked with mild laughter. "You getting too old for it," he said.

"Go to hell, *viejo*," said Nathan, batting at the dust on his clothes. He winced at the pain in his shoulder, which he'd damned near dislocated in that fall.

"Too old, Nate. How old you getting to be, eh? Twenty-nine? Thirty?"

"Twenty-eight. As you damned well know."

"Too old, too old," old Cruz sing-songed. "Man's bones brittle up when he passes twenty-five. After that, is no good to be rough-busting *ladinos*. One day you get busted to pieces."

Sandal said, "*Abuelito*, when can I start to rough-bust 'em?"

"That's up to Nate. Hell, he's the great *jinete* of horsemen around here." Diego patted his grandson's shoulder. "Me, I been turned out to pasture."

Nathan smiled at Sandal's questioning look. Slim and wiry at sixteen, Sandal was Nathan's protégé much as Nathan had been Diego's before him. "You have plenty of time," he told the boy. "Get a little more heft on your bones. You're too light, Sandal."

Old Diego cocked his head, old eyes sparkling wickedly. "Heh, heh. You take another turn at the *ladino*, no?"

Nathan shook his head. "Not today. The big boss and I are going for a ride."

Probably Diego was right, he thought, feeling the insistent tug of pain in his back and shoulder as he and Sandal roped and snubbed the mustang, then stripped off the saddle. It was a lot harder to ride out the kinks once a man lost the green and supple bones of youth. He might have to give up on the dun. Or have a professional horsebreaker brought in to take his rough edges off. Nathan

64

hated that idea: It was the old story of a man's pride.

Ty Banner had limped up to the corral in time to catch the furious action as the mustang bucked himself out. He had sketchbook and pencil in hand, and now he was sitting on an upended crate and rapidly sketching, his loose-fleshed face firmed in a scowl of concentration.

As Nathan and Sandal came out of the corral, Ty said savagely, "Shit!" and tore the page out of his sketchbook, balled it in a fist and flung it aside.

Sandal recovered the crumpled sheet and smoothed it out. His big dark eyes glistened with awe as he gazed at the discarded sketch. "Señor Ty, tha's a beautiful picture. How come you throw it away?"

"It's a piece of shit, that's why." Ty heaved himself to his feet with the aid of his crutch. "What the hell qualifies you as an art critic all at once?"

"I don' know nothing about that, but boy, I know what I like." Sandal showed the sketch to Nathan. "Hey, ain' that som'thing, Nate?"

It was. Ty had drawn the mustang at the height of a twisting sunfish—minus his rider. With an amazing economy of bold swift strokes, he had captured the wild, feral power of the animal and the moment.

"Can I keep it?" Sandal asked in a reverent tone. "I wan' to hang it on my wall."

"I don't give a good damn if you run it through a coffee mill and cook it up for breakfast with chili peppers."

"Good! Thank you." Sandal hurried after his grandfather, who was heading toward the log shanty they shared, not far from Nathan's. "Hey, *Abuelito*! Look what Señor Ty give me."

Ty sent a baleful glance after him, then began slapping the pockets of his belted Norfolk-tweed jacket. He produced a silver flask from one pocket, eyed it with a twitch of his lips, then returned it to the pocket.

"Too early even for you, eh?" Nathan asked.

"Go to half-breed hell, why don't you?" Ty groped in another pocket and took out a box of the Turkish cigarettes he'd ordered from a Chicago tobacconist. He lighted one up and took a deep long drag on it.

Nathan said, "I'd think having an admirer would cheer even you up."

"Sure. Greaser kids are natural art critics. All shit-lovers are." A few more drags on his cigarette mollified Ty a little. He eyed Nathan critically. "You took a nasty spill there, old hoss."

Nathan gave a wry shrug. It made him wince; he rubbed his shoulder. "Guess it's like Diego says. A man gets on."

"Then tell my old man to hire someone else for that part of it. Screw your pride."

Nathan grinned. "Maybe I will."

He and Ty remained friends, in spite of the differences the passing years had drawn between them. Ty had been the first to make him feel welcome on that long-gone day when he'd first come to Swallowtail: a scared, bewildered kid of six, torn from what few roots he'd known, dragged along on foot for freezing miles by a mother who'd never given him a gentle word. It was the Ty Banner of their boyhood days that Nathan remembered with affection: bright and sensitive, moody and buoyant, often hard to understand. But always a friend. Taking Nathan's side against his own big brother, Thorp, and getting knocked bloody for it more than once.

Once in a while that fresh and idealistic boy still glimmered through the savage bitterness that Ty wore around his old sensibilities, a shell that was in some ways like the gross and sluggish flesh that encased his still-youthful body. Not often, but sometimes. That, and the memories, made Nathan tolerant of Ty's ascerbic ways—especially in early morning. You couldn't expect Ty to belt it down the way he did and still greet the dawn as perky as a wren.

One hopeful sign, lately, was that Ty had begun tinkering with his art once more. On the other hand, he was so savagely dissatisfied with everything he attempted that you wondered if it were for the best, after all. . . .

Nathan glanced toward the main house, set on

a long slope well above the working quarters. Ike and Thorp had stepped off the veranda and were heading this way, Thorp accommodating his long-legged walk to his father's stumpy, arthritic one.

They were having another heated exchange of words. No doubt a continuation of yesterday's squabble.

Nathan went to the harness shed and got his own saddle and Ike's, and lugged them out to the corral gate. By this time Ike and Thorp had arrived at the corral and halted there, still wrangling. Ty stood by, listening with a sardonic amusement.

Nathan roped out Ike's big bay and cinched on the special saddle. It was a rig that Diego Cruz had devised for the big boss, whose arthritic condition made riding a perilous business for him. To assure that Ike would be firmly seated, Diego had sewed a harness of inch-wide leather straps to the hull. Equipped with buckles and awl-punched holes, the straps could be cinched like belts around Ike's upper legs and lower trunk, anchoring him securely to the saddle. Even if his horse got fractious, he couldn't lose his seat. Nathan whistled up and saddled his own piebald, and led both animals out of the corral. Ike and Thorp had fallen silent now, ignoring each other.

Ike grasped the reins that Nathan handed him.

His once-powerful hands were still immense, but gnarled and joint-swollen. Thorp made no move to help as Nathan gave the old man a boost into his saddle; then secured the straps in place. Hands fisted painfully around the reins, Ike stared grimly down at his eldest son.

"You don't need to like it," he said. "Just mind what I told you before. I want those three assholes out of that line camp and off my land by tonight. That clear enough for you?"

"Clear as springwater."

"You'll need to replace 'em with a couple men from our crew."

"I will. Just one thing, Pa."

"What's that?"

Thorp stood with his big fists cocked on his hips, an arrogant jut to his jaw. "From now on, I have the say on who I'll put on that duty or any other. And who I keep on it. Otherwise, you know what you can do with your goddamn foreman's job."

Thorp let his hands fall to his sides and waited for Ike's answer, braced for it.

But Ike only lifted his reins and said mildly, "Fair enough," as he put his horse in motion.

He and Nathan rode away from the headquarters. For maybe a quarter mile, Ike held a brooding silence. Then he said abruptly, "I ain't been doing a right job of dealing with Thorp. Come down to it, maybe I never have."

Nathan didn't figure that called for any comment. But Ike glanced at him then, and Nathan let his shoulders lift and settle. "I have lived as close to your family as anyone has," he said. "I don't see what you could have done that was any better."

"Neither do I," Ike said wearily. "But Jesus, Nate. I'm his pa. I ought to of found a way."

CHAPTER 5

Ike was an old man and his health was going downhill year by year. Most times when he thought about his father, Thorp Banner thought of him in just that way. The point being: Ike couldn't have too many years remaining to him. That kind of thinking used to bother Thorp a little. More recently, he hadn't bothered to deny to himself that the old man's death would give his own fortunes a convenient upturn.

Not that Thorp ever considered hurrying the process along. If the notion did flicker across his mind once in a while, it was swiftly and impatiently buried. Thorp could be pretty dispassionate about most things, even priding himself on the fact. But a murderer he wasn't, and Ike was his pa. A pretty damn right sort of Pa too—always had been. Thorp held no festering rancors of any kind toward him.

All the same, it was hard not to think now and then about the attendant benefits for Thorp Banner if the old man were to quietly drop dead one day. As he probably would, given time. The big question was: How long would it take?

Riding across Swallowtail's northwest range on this sun-washed morning, Thorp did as much hard thinking on the possibility as he ever had. As usual, he put it finally and implacably out of mind. He had a sizable problem to get shed of . . . but no answer lay in that direction.

What he needed was a way to cover his tracks. And just maybe he had it.

At first his show of being fired up at Ike's ultimatum demanding that he get rid of the Purleys had been almost genuine. Thorp never let his temper get out of control, but at times it was handy to let people think it was. It gave a kind of righteous edge to any posture of indignation he assumed. But after he'd thought about the ultimatum awhile, even his own cold, private resentment had died.

Yessir . . . firing the Purleys might be the answer to his dilemma.

It was almost noon when Thorp rode into the long wooded valley where the line camp was. He crossed it and came onto a cleared flat. The shack and the building were old and weathered, built of peeled logs. They were starting to get a tumbledown look, and the fences were in need of repair. That fact told as much about the camp's present tenants as did the bottles and rusting tin cans that littered the yard.

Thorp was anything but fastidious in his person, but his working habits were tidy. He had his moment of profound disgust as he rode across the yard. Damn stinking hill trash, he thought. Give 'em a month in a place, and it's gone to a sty.

He wasn't surprised, either, that at midday when they should be out at work, the three Purleys were loafing around the camp. Claud was stretched on his back on the porch, hands folded across his belly and hat tipped over his eyes. Sheb was sitting on the step, moodily hacking at the edge of it with a hunting knife while he watched his pa practice with the bullwhip.

Snake had set up a row of tin cans on a fence rail and was knocking them off with dexterous strokes of his whip. He was pretty good at it. He would send the whip snapping out to its full length, and just about every time the shot-weighted tip would smack a can dead center and send it flying. The impact was enough to deeply indent the can.

Seeing Thorp now, he paused and unhurriedly coiled his whip, offering that sly, smart-ass grin of his. "How do there, Mr. Banner," he sang out.

Thorp stepped out of his saddle and snapped his fingers at Sheb. "You," he said, "take care of my horse. Walk him a spell. Then water him."

Sheb rose uncertainly to his feet, scowling. He glanced at his pa and got Snake's tolerant nod before slouching over and taking the reins from Thorp's hand.

"Glory to goodness," Snake said, around a cheekful of plug-cut. "You must excuse us. We was not expecting company."

73

"Good thing you told me," said Thorp. "No way I would of guessed."

He took off his hat and mopped the sweatband with his bandanna as he walked over to Snake. Clamping his hat on again, he held out his hand. "Mind if I have a look at that?"

Snake's eyes narrowed. He turned his head and carefully spat and then, reluctantly, handed Thorp his coiled-up whip.

Thorp shook it out and ran an eye along its sinuous length. "This sure is a thing," he said admiringly. "Snake, I am afraid I got bad news for you and your boys."

"What's 'at?"

"My pa is on the peck over what you fellows did to that siwash Injun yesterday. He says to dispense with your services."

"Heh?"

"I'm supposed to fire you."

"Well, glory to hard days!" Snake said angrily, and spat again. "If that don't tear the rag offen the bush. When you hired us Purleys on and give this camp into our keeping, you said we was to give a good rousting to any Indins we found over this way. Any reason we could find would do, you said."

Thorp nodded tranquilly. For years he had violently objected to Ike's permitting that harum-scarum band of Jack Lynch's to squat on their northern range, but to no effect. Thorp had assigned the Purleys to the nearby line camp in hopes that they might trump up a pretense, any kind at all, that would compel Ike to quit defending Lynch's bunch and enable Thorp to drive them off the land.

Yesterday might have provided the excuse, if Nathan hadn't come along and witnessed the whole thing. Ike was bound to take that breed's word over anyone else's, any day.

Snake's face was ruddy with temper. Claud had gotten to his feet and was standing in a kind of ominous slouch, thumbs hooked in his belt. Sheb blinked sullenly at Thorp and then dropped his horse's reins.

Tongue firmly in his cheek, Thorp grinned at all of them. "That's what I had in mind," he agreed. "But Nate Drew has gummed up the works for us." He waggled the whipstock. "Say, you mind if I take a shot with this thing?"

Not waiting for a reply, he sent the whip peeling out three times in quick succession. Two cans were knocked flying from the corral pole, bent almost double by the force of the lead popper. The third can was only struck at the rim, but that was enough to send it spinning end over end.

"Huh." Thorp shook his head regretfully. "Must be losing my touch. No slight intended to this here whip of yours, Snake. Damn fine whip. Man can knock down three in a row with it, he has got to allow it's one damn fine whip."

His gaze touched idly on each Purley in turn. Sheb picked up the reins again. Claud grunted and leaned his shoulder against a porch post, looking bored. Snake began slowly to work the cud of plug-cut in his jaw, and did not spit.

"Anyways," Thorp went on, "my old man plays the tune, and I reckon we got to dance to it. Afraid you boys will have to skedaddle like he says. Only maybe not very far."

Snake eyed him carefully. "What's 'at mean?"

They were ready to listen now, and Thorp didn't waste words. He talked swiftly, punching words home like fists.

Thorp's weakness was gambling. Generally he kept the fever in check except when he made the mistake of mixing cards and liquor. Then it raged out of control. That's what had happened a couple weeks ago over in Cold River, nearest town to the east of here. After taking aboard more whiskey than he could safely handle, Thorp had dropped all his money and then run up a huge debt in a private high-stakes poker game.

Thorp needed money in a hurry. He could hold his creditors at bay by paying them off a little at a time, but even that means of squaring his account would take more than he could lay hands on at present. Meantime those creditors were growing impatient; they'd made clear that if they couldn't collect their winnings from him, they'd take his I.O.U.s to his pa. And that would be disastrous for Thorp Banner.

In his younger, wilder days he had run up so many gambling debts that Ike, after paying them off, had flatly warned him that one more escapade of the sort would get him cut from Ike's will. Knowing Ike would keep his word, Thorp had since avoided all but games for penny-ante stakes. When unfuddled by liquor, he was a shrewd and careful player who won more often than he lost.

Now, one drunken and profligate fling with the cards threatened to cost him not only his birthright but the foremanship of Swallowtail as well. That would be like the old man—to break him down to a common crewman. And Thorp knew that if it happened, his arrogant pride would force him to quit Swallowtail for good.

He was goddamned if he'd let that happen. If he could hang on for the few years Ike had left, Swallowtail would be his. To be shared with two brothers: That was the bitter pill he had to swallow. But he could dominate Free with ease; it would put as good as a two-thirds interest in his hands. Unless Ike were to split up the ranch proper among the three of them. The old man had never revealed the contents of his will, and so it remained a possibility. But Thorp would take that chance.

He didn't lay it out for the Purleys in nearly

that much detail. He said just enough to apprise them of his need for money.

"That's where you come in," he told Ike. "You boys are going to fetch me in the money. Line your own pockets too."

Snake's eyes glinted with suspicion. "How's 'at?"

"There's a town just across the Palisades. Place known as Caldwell. It has got a spur line to a main railroad and facilities for shipping out cattle."

"I heerd of it."

What they were going to do, Thorp explained, was run off jags of Swallowtail cows and move them across the Palisades to Caldwell. He and the Purleys would split the proceeds down the middle. Ordinarily, Swallowtail shipped its beef out of Cold River. It wasn't as close as Caldwell, but pushing cattle across the rugged Palisades made for a sight tougher drive. Nevertheless, it could be done. Thorp would lay out the route himself. The important thing was that his pa had always carried on all his business dealings in Cold River, never in Caldwell. Wasn't much danger of any sales of Swallowtail cattle in Caldwell leaking back to Ike through his old-time business associates. It had been a long while, in any case, since Ike had been able to handle much on the business end of ranch affairs.

"With three of you working the brush back in

these foothills," Thorp went on, "you can round up enough cows to make it worth the while. Won't take more'n you three to trail small bunches of 'em to Caldwell. Nothing big at one time, see? Them cows won't be missed till the spring tally. Then it'll be blamed on a heavy winterkill or on them Navajos at Lynchtown. By that time you'll be long out of the country with a couple thousand in cash lining your pockets. Me, I'll have my gambling losses paid off. How's it sound?"

Snake's face squinched up into crafty lines. You could almost smell his greed warring with his caution as he silently debated the proposition.

"Sniff 'er over from all sides," Thorp smiled, coiling up the whip in his big hands. "It's sound as a dollar, way I have figured it."

"We'll see, now," murmured Snake. "You're pitching us out o' this place. Where we supposed to go and live?"

"You'll lay low in an old trapper's cabin I know of back in the hills. It ain't far from here. Been deserted for years."

"Ain't far from here," Snake echoed. "But once you put us out o' this line camp, you will put other men in it. They will be in a handy way to spot any cow-lifting goes on."

"Huh-uh." Playfully, Thorp lifted Snake's hat off his head. He dropped the coiled whip over Snake's neck, then plunked the hat back on, giving it a rakish tilt. "They won't spot nothing 'cause they won't be looking. I am putting in two guys from our own crew who I can trust to look t'other way. That's if I slip a little bonus in their pay pokes every month. Why, damn it, Snake, you can lift cows hereabouts the year long and feel as safe as if you was back in your mammy's arms."

"Sure," Snake said softly. "Only just how is it we supposed to peddle wet cattle that near to Swallowtail when Swallowtail is a brand knowed all over the Territory? If you don't usually sell no beef there, any cattle buyer we come at from over the Palisades will be on a caution for fair. He will be suspicious of vented brands."

"Why," Thorp said amiably, "you ain't gonna vent no brands on these here beeves, you old weasel you. They will wear the Swallowtail brand, all nice and legal. I have got a cattle buyer lined up in Caldwell who won't ask no questions long as there ain't no risk to his hide. And there won't be. I will sign the bills of lading myself, and you will take 'em to railhead with the cows."

"Huh. You can do that?"

"Sure. I got Pa's power-of-attorney. He give it to me after the arthritis took him so bad he couldn't get around enough to conduct hardly any of his own business. He is stuck on Swallowtail most all the time now . . . and I manage most all our dealings."

"Glory to goodness," Snake murmured, shaking his head. "Ain't that a nice thing for you."

Thorp grinned. "What you'll do, you will give my man in Caldwell a bill of lading made out all nice and proper by the Swallowtail foreman, and he will pay you for the cows and not let out a peep. It will be a purely legal transaction."

"You be a trusting man, Mr. Banner."

"Hand over *your* share of the money, I meant. He will hold my half for me and I will collect it later."

Snake's shoulders jerked with an appreciative little chuckle. "So we can trust each other down the line, hey? Mr. Banner, you have got all your tracks covered, seems like. Ours too. Sounds right peart, and I am minded to take up your proposal."

He glanced at his older son. "Well, you heerd it. How does it set in your craw?"

Claud shrugged. "I reckon good enough. Anyways, I allus go by your say-so."

"By grab, yes. You do. Give your tail a twist now and then and you jump right smart, Claud."

"What about the horse-holder, there?" asked Thorp. "He don't look too sure."

Snake shook his head sadly. "Mr. Banner, you have got to make allowances for my boy Sheb, which is about the dumbest son of a bitch the Lord has seen fit to grace his green earth with.

Sheb will chirp when I say cricket. That is all a man can ask."

Sheb's eyes flickered with a sullen smolder. He said nothing.

Still lounging against the post, Claud laughed. "He is got enough smarts under his hat to tell if he is being shit on, Pappy. You got to give him that."

Sheb wheeled suddenly, dropping the reins again. His face blazed with a naked ferocity; his hunting knife flashed out of its sheath at his hip. It made a silvery arc in the sun. The blade embedded a third of its length in the porch post about two inches from Claud's arm.

Claud leaped sideways as if he'd been stung. "Why you bug-house bastard!" he hollered. "I'll—"

"You won't nothing," Snake cut in tolerantly. "You simmer down now, the both of you." He glanced blandly at Thorp. "He could a set that sticker right smack in Claud's flesh just as easy. He is got a bug under his bonnet, that boy, but he is some shuckins with a knife."

Thorp was grinning at this byplay; he let the grin widen. "I appreciate that," he said. "Something for a man to bear in mind, huh?"

CHAPTER 6

Ike Banner liked to reminisce about the territory's early days. He was in that kind of a mood this morning, as he and Nathan Drew rode toward his north range and Lynchtown.

Ike hadn't been much more than a kid back then, in those last days of the old mountain men. He had known just about all the great ones: Carson, Bridger, "Broken Hand" Fitzpatrick, "Old Bill" Williams. But all of those fellows had been coming long in the tooth even then, survivors of a still younger day. The great rendezvous that used to gather in the old-time hivernants, laden with their winter's caches of furs, had already been a thing of the past.

Ike and Angus Drew and Jack Lynch had been among the last of the breed, and pickings were pretty slim by that time. The three youthful partners had gloried in the life all the same. The territory still belonged to Mexico then, and a man could still find the flavor of Old Spain and the *mestizo* culture. God, what a life it had been for three young fellows coming of age! They'd trapped the mountain streams, wading out in the icy water, recovering and skinning beaver carcasses. Through long evenings they would scrape and stretch the hides on curing frames. Come spring, they would pack them down to sell to the traders at Santa Fe and sometimes at Taos.

Ike remembered how the *pulque* and *tequila* burned sweetly down a man's throat and how good a brown, warm, plump *señorita* could be. He remembered it through a dreaming haze of nostalgia. Nathan had heard it all before, and he knew not all of it had been so good. He suspected that Ike knew it too, but he never tired of hearing the stories as Ike told them.

They had been inseparable in those days—Ike and Angus and Jack. Three friends with a lot of high hard living behind them and nothing but eager expectations ahead of them. War with Mexico had ended that carefree life. All three had enlisted as scouts with the U. S. Army, and after it was over and the territory was ceded to the U. S., each had gone his own way.

Jack Lynch had gone to live with the Navajo, marrying into the tribe and wholly adopting its way of life. Angus Drew had stayed with the army, rising to the position of Chief of Scouts at Fort Stamford. But as a native of Georgia, he had quit the service when the War of the Rebellion came, and then—refusing to fight against old comrades—had gone to hunt up his old partner Jack. He too had joined up with the Navajo, soon becoming the husband of Jack's young niece, Horse Woman.

Ike Banner had gone gold-hunting in Arizona and had made a strike that had enabled him to acquire a sizable chunk of the mountain country he had hunted and trapped as a youth. He'd met and courted and wed Luella Breakenridge, and had settled down to develop Swallowtail. When the war broke out, he'd enlisted with Major John Chivington's First Colorado Volunteers, only to be cut down by a Minié ball in the regiment's first engagement with Confederate forces, at Apache Canyon near Santa Fe.

"That Chivington was a Scripture-spouting hypocrite bastard," Ike said meditatively. "Hated Indians worse'n my boy Thorp does. You heard of what he done at Sand Creek? Sure you have. But God, was that man a fighter. Larruped the asses off those rebs. Anyways, the war was over for me and I was invalided home to Luella. Thorp was coming five that spring. Growed like a weed while I was gone. Cute little fella. Well, I reckon even he couldn't help starting that way."

Nathan grinned. "Guess you didn't stay invalided very long."

"Nope. Now look here, Nate. I ever told you any of this before, you be sure and let me know."

Nathan returned Ike's sober wink with an equally sober nod.

"Fine. Like you say, I got an itchy foot pretty quick. Thought I would hunt up my old partners, Jack and Angus. Well, it took some hunting right enough, but I found 'em. They was living with their wives' family, the Many Hogans Clan, in the valley of the Rio Grande del Norte."

Ike seemed to slip into a gray musing then, and finally Nathan felt obliged to break the silence. "That was the last time you saw my pa, wasn't it?"

Ike roused himself with an effort. "Yeah. Last time I seen old Angus. I stayed a month with the band and then went home. Was over seven years before I seen Jack Lynch again."

Nathan remembered that time well enough. It had been some eight months after that icy, blowing day in the fall of 1869 that Horse Woman and he had stumbled into Swallowtail, half-starved and nearly frozen to death. As the widow and son of Ike's old friend, they had found a warm welcome. Nobody at the ranch had been kinder or more hospitable than Luella Banner.

From Horse Woman, Ike had learned the fate of the Many Hogans people. Late in 1862, shortly after Ike's visit to the Rio Grande del Norte, Colonel Kit Carson and his mixed army of regulars and volunteers had rounded up the main body of the Navajo nation at its traditional stronghold of Canyon de Chelly and had sent them to the bottomlands of the Corn River to become peaceful herders and farmers. The Many Hogans Clan, too, had been exiled there, and like their Navajo brothers had come near to extinction after their removal from their ancestral cliff and mesa country in the Painted Desert.

A final bitter blow had fallen when the U. S. Government had sold the Navajos' Corn River lands to the railroad. At that time the Many Hogans Clan had split away from the main tribe and had made its way to timber country in the mountainous north. Here, in a pocket of wilderness far from the influence of the *Belinkana* and their army, all had gone well for the *Dineh*—the People—in seasons when the hunting was good and the weather was warm and ripe for crops. But the particularly severe winter of 1868–69 had almost wiped out the clan. Its members were ill-suited for a spring of chill weather and drizzling rains that lasted through that summer and into fall. By then the Navajos were dying like flies.

Angus Drew had shared the fate of dozens of his Indian comrades, coming down with pneumonia and sinking into swift decline. After his death, Horse Woman had made her decision to depart the clan with her six-year-old son, traveling countless miles to reach Swallowtail ranch and throw them on the mercy of her husband's old friend, Ike Banner.

Horse Woman and her son had remained on Swallowtail till the following spring, when Ike Banner escorted the two back to the Many Hogans village. The winter had taken a bitter toll of the remaining clan members, and it was for this reason that Jack Lynch—who was now leader of the clan—had heeded Ike's urgings to move his band to a better location. Ike had offered a permanent refuge on his northern range, and had promised assistance whenever they might need it. And Ike had had Angus Drew's remains brought to the little cemetery on Swallowtail.

Lynchtown, the village came to be called. Its existence on his range had brought heavy criticism on Ike over the years. The big ranchers were used to dealing swiftly and ruthlessly with Indian "squatters," even if those same Indians had occupied the same land long before the whites. Ike had a headful of wrong-headed notions, they claimed, and Lynchtown was about as sorry a proof of it as you could ask for.

There was something to be said for the accusation. Nathan Drew, who had spent all but his first six years at Swallowtail headquarters, only visiting Lynchtown from time to time, had to admit it.

Still—what in hell did the whites expect? You couldn't undercut the entire culture of a people and expect to breed archangels. The web of tenuous connections that existed between the Navajo and his earth wasn't merely a whole and complex system, subtle and infinite beyond any white man's comprehension, it was also incredibly fragile, swiftly contaminated by any contact with an outside culture.

In a couple decades, Lynchtown had grown in the way that unnatural things sometimes did, spreading like a blight across the green valley of its location. Homeless drifters, Indians and part-bloods, the shiftless off-scourings of a dozen tribes, were drawn to a place where a once-proud clan of the *Dineh* could live pridelessly off the bounty of a benevolent overlord who would let them hunt and herd and farm as they pleased. And who'd provide for them in needy times, too. Children were born and grew up in a polyglot and confused situation, picking up every vice known to man before they were ten. Over half the able-bodied males were chronic drinkers—of their own homemade distillings or whatever they could pack in from outside.

Lynchtown was a mess, all right. If Ike ever regretted what he had begun with such fair intentions, he never said so. Nathan had never asked. Probably Ike figured that, willy-nilly, Lynchtown was his responsibility, one he couldn't just abandon at this late date.

The trouble was: What would happen to that sad lot of people when Ike was gone? Because of his blood ties there, the question bothered Nathan Drew a good deal. Yet like Ike, and like Jack Lynch himself, he was helpless when it came to providing any sort of answer. . . .

Some of this, anyway, was pressing on Ike's thoughts at the same time. Not looking at Nathan, he said abruptly, "Nate, what's to become of Swallowtail after I pass over?"

"Hard one to answer," Nathan said carefully. "There's a lot of things might happen."

Ike gave a mirthless chuckle. "Which says purely nothing, and maybe you're right. A man owes his blood something, and I got to see my sons get their due. But hell . . . leave the outfit in their joint care? It'll set 'em at each other's throats sure. Anyways, Ty won't ever make any kind of a cattleman."

"I reckon not," Nathan said in a neutral voice.

Ike had grown to a tolerance of his middle son that he'd never had when Ty was a kid. Nathan was well aware that Ike's guilty sense of having pushed the boy in a wrong direction was what now caused him to wink at Ty's heavy drinking. The blow of Aunt Lu's death had taken something out of Ike. It had mellowed him too greatly, Nathan often thought; nowadays Ike tolerated too much.

Yesterday, it was true, he had disciplined Thorp. But he had a groping, uncertain opinion about the wisdom of his own action. This was nothing like the Ike Banner of old, and Nathan didn't like to see it.

"And Thorp," Ike went on musingly. "He's waiting on just one thing. The day I give up the ghost. He's waiting on that so hard, he can taste it."

That surprised Nathan a little. So Ike had seen it too. Yet Nathan made no comment.

"No argument, huh?" Ike's humorless laugh again. "Right. There ain't any."

He talks to me a lot, thought Nathan, and he doesn't talk much to anyone else. Nathan liked that, even if he didn't like a lot of what Ike said these days.

It hadn't always been that way. Far from it. After Horse Woman had first brought her son to Swallowtail, Ike had seemed actually to avoid him. Later on he'd taken a gruff notice of the growing boy, assigning Nathan to Diego Cruz's watchful tutelage, and in falls and winters sending him to Cold River where he'd gotten a better-than-fair education from a private school-master who'd boarded young scholars at his small academy. But only recently had Ike Banner, old and lonely now, grown truly close to the half-breed waif he'd taken in because of his friendship for Nathan Drew's dead father.

The land tended upward as the two men rode. For a long time they followed the old trace that led to the cemetery, then cut away from it toward the northwest. Now the foothills of the Palisades undulated into valleys and rises where heavy timber vied with open meadows.

They were crossing the stony ribbon of a dried-up

stream bed when the shot came. It whined off a rock a few yards away and sent the horses into a mild panic.

Ike grated, "What the hell!" as he hauled up his dancing mount.

Nathan said flatly, "Move! Get out of here!" And caught Ike's rein as he gigged his own horse forward, yanking Ike's animal into motion too.

They pounded across the damp stream bed and took the steep, willow-choked bank in a lunging climb, crashing into the brush. Another slug bored through the foliage, clipping off twigs and leaves.

More open ground lay beyond the streamside brush, and Nathan didn't attempt to cross it. He braced the horses to a halt in the thick of the dense willow growth and dropped out of his saddle, and started to unharness Ike from his.

"Damn it, boy!" Ike yelled. "Don't get us stuck here. Let's make a run—"

A third bullet slashed through the willows, and this one seared the rump of Ike's bay. The animal humped into a wild pitching; Nathan had to grab his headstall to haul him down. If Ike hadn't been cinched on, he would have taken a nasty tumble.

With the bay almost steadied down, Nathan snapped, "Hold him!" Ike swore, but fisted his arthritic hands fast around the reins.

"You stay right here and you stay down low," Nathan told Ike as he attacked the harness again, swiftly undoing straps. "Any way we break out, we'd make plain targets. Not much cover here, but there's some. . . ."

He pulled Ike almost bodily off the bay and down behind a shallow fringe of boulders along the stream bank. It made for a slight shelter, but the willow brush would help screen them if they stayed low enough.

Good enough for Ike, thought Nathan as he quickly knotted the reins of both horses to a thick-stemmed willow. For his own part, Nathan had no intention of remaining pinned here. He'd fixed the direction of the first two shots; they had come from a rocky hillside to the east. On the third shot, he had seen a black-powder smear of smoke fraying away from the hill's summit. No great range for a man with a good rifle, unless he was a pretty bad shot. Or he might have fired to frighten, not to kill.

Either way, whoever it was wanted a lesson taught him. And no matter what his intent had been, Nathan wanted to learn the reason for this ambush.

"You stay here," he told Ike. *"And keep down!"*

"Damn it, who you think you're—!"

But Nathan was already fading away through the brush, his rifle in hand. He'd reinforced its split stock with strips of wet rawhide that had dried and tightened to an ironlike binding, and he thought it would hold all right.

Ducking as low as he could and moving almost in dead silence, Nathan used both rocks and brush to hide his movements. He worked swiftly north along the bank, clinging to its cover. And thought maybe he was passing unseen by the man on the hill, until a bullet sang off a huge boulder not a yard from him.

Nathan dived behind the boulder, hugging its weathered scaling flank. He sent a swift glance up and down the stream bed and across it. About another fifty yards upstream an arm of young firs protruded from a greater body of timber that lay north and east of his present position. If he could get inside that pocket of firs, he'd be out of this damned trap. And would be on even terms, at least, with the enemy.

Trouble was, he'd have to cross at least ten yards of open ground at the narrowest distance that lay between the bank willows and the firs. But to reach that point, he'd have to worm his way through this scanty brush for another long, aching interval. . . .

It never did a man's nerve any good to think too long on such decisions. Once Nathan knew what he would do, he moved swiftly. Fixed his mind on his goal and not on the fact that a bullet might find him at any moment. He ran, crouched, twisted, and sometimes half-crawled his way along the bank. Again the unseen man's slugs seemed to search him out. But never to kill.

Lead pummeled the earth close to Nathan's feet; lead sent flakes of tattered leaves dusting over him. Once, particles of flying rock from a ricochet stung his hand. Seven shots were fired in all. Each came terrifyingly near him, and not one touched him.

That was no accident!

Reaching the point where the fir trees lay nearest, Nathan flung himself to the ground between a sizable pair of rocks. His right hand was bleeding where the fragments had struck. Absently he licked the blood from his knuckles as he studied the lay of those fir trees.

Yes . . . all that timber should give him plenty of concealment. If he got that far. *Would the rifleman let him?* Again, he thought fast and acted at once.

Nathan sprang to his feet and into the open, hurtling across the intervening space; his feet digging wildly to left and right as he tried to zigzag in his run. There was no need. No shots came. He reached the canopy of close-growing firs and dropped face down on the bare earth inside their deep cover. His heart pounded wildly; he was shaking all over. His hands were slick with sweat and blood.

In a few seconds Nathan rose slowly to his feet, his lips peeling back off his teeth. *Let's see who does the sweating now!*

During his adolescence he had spent quite a lot

of time visiting with the Navajos of Lynchtown. The blood of the Many Hogans Clan had still run fairly clean in those days. Men who knew the old skills had been willing to instruct him in the fine points of woodcraft. Nathan had learned how to follow track of all kinds, how to move like a ghost in brush and timber. A man didn't forget such lessons. Once learned, they were bred into the bone of him.

The heat of Nathan's anger burned away to a hard coldness. Quickly and silently, he prowled along the cramped aisles of the firs and into the greater stand of timber, where he skirted wide through the trees in order to work up back of the rocky hill from which the shots had come.

He'd have to move fast if he were to intercept the rifleman. Now that the enemy had lost sight of him, he was certain to change his position as swiftly as possible. Try an ambush from a different spot. Or he would make a hasty retreat. Nathan didn't want him to escape any more than he wanted to shoot the fellow. What he wanted was answers.

This close to Lynchtown, it stood to reason that one of its inhabitants had deadfalled Ike and him. Whoever it was must have spotted them by pure chance . . . but hadn't hesitated to use this opportunity to give them a bad scare. That alone argued that a Lynchtowner had fired at them to express resentment for the treatment that had been accorded Jimmy Hosteen. And if it were young Adakhai who had spread the word, you could damned well be sure the whole incident had lost nothing in the telling. . . .

Nathan came out of the woods on the back flank of the hill. He stopped at forest's edge, his gaze sweeping the bare rock-studded slope. Somebody might still be laid up in that nest of boulders at its crown, but the odds were he had cleared out by now.

Holding his rifle up and ready, Nathan went up the slope at a diagonal, moving at a swift trot and watching the ground as much as the upper hill. He pulled to a stop, seeing the clear impress of a heel mark on a patch of soft earth. And another beyond it.

The ambusher had come off the slope at a hard run, retreating toward the trees below and to the near south. The direction of his run was clear. Nathan wheeled and headed that way, loping toward the front line of trees. Even as he did, he heard the sound of a running horse inside the grove.

Nathan plunged into the trees. He had caught a fleeting glimpse of a dun pony, a dark figure flattened against its mane, the flash of a red bandanna. Now he yelled after the fellow and fired above his head.

It failed to slow him. In a moment the woods swallowed the horse and rider; the roll of hoofbeats ebbed away into the ordinary sounds of the forest.

Nathan swore once. Almost dispassionately, as he'd half-expected this might happen. On foot now, he couldn't give immediate chase. By the time he fetched his own mount and picked up the trail, the rider would have a wide lead on him.

Maybe Lynchtown was the place to look for answers.

CHAPTER 7

Lynchtown was located in a great natural bowl of a valley surrounded by guardian cliffs. In places the ancient granite heights had crumbled away in chunky slides that a man or animal could scale with some difficulty. The inhabitants grazed their flocks of goats and woolies in adjoining valleys, for the Lynchtown bowl was taken up, in addition to shacks and hogans, by fields of corn and potatoes, beans and squash.

A wide notch at the bowl's south end gave ingress to it. This entrance was flanked by spires of rock where the clan used to post sentries by day and night . . . back in those days when the people still worried about the U. S. Army or a posse of wrathful white civilians coming to roust them out. That danger had seemed to dwindle over the years, and with the settling of the clan into slack and degenerate ways, they'd long ago ceased to mount guards.

Today, though, as Nathan Drew and Ike Banner approached the pass, they saw a lone man at the summit of one gaunt finger of rock. He was armed with a rifle and he did not hail them, only watched unmoving as they rode through the notch into the bowl.

Maybe the sound of those ambush shots had

made the Lynchtowners nervous. Or they were expecting that the whipping of Jimmy Hosteen would bring more trouble on its heels.

Nathan and Ike were greeted by a bedlam of yapping dogs and a crowd of silent people. Many of the older Navajos had known Nathan since boyhood; they had been on friendly terms with Ike Banner for years. If not for that, the mood might have been genuinely hostile. It wasn't exactly friendly, even so. The two men rode slowly through the village, saying a pleasant, "*Ahalani, anaai!*" here and there: "Greetings, brother!"

Some answered, but with a wary reserve.

A few of the hogans were of the traditional kind: forked-together homes whose structure had been decreed by the Talking God. A number of other dwellings, logs-stacked-up houses built of piñon logs and cedar bark, showed the white man's influence. And there were nondescript shacks and outbuildings thrown carelessly together out of whatever materials were at hand.

Jack Lynch and his woman lived in a hogan that hewed to the old style. He came out to greet his visitors, raising a hand palm out.

A tall and angular man, Jack Lynch was still erect and unstooped at seventy-two. He wore a jacket of red wool and rawhide leggings buttoned at the knees; silver ornaments clashed softly to his movements. His gray hair was worn in two squashlike knots at the back of his head. It was amazing to realize how Navajo this born Irishman had come to look over the years.

"*Xoxo naxasi, natani,*" Nathan said gravely. "*So ah hayai, bike-hazanai.*"

He gave the greeting reserved for a chief, and the wishing him a long and happy life, because he knew it would please Jack Lynch. A twinkle touched the old man's blue eyes as he answered just as gravely, "*Ahalani, shiyaazh.* Greetings, my son."

Nathan had always felt the conflicts in his own diverse heritage. No such doubts troubled Jack Lynch. He was one of those few whites who had accomplished the incredible, turning completely Indian within themselves. It involved an adjustment far more complex than just getting the language and customs down pat. Jack Lynch had come to move and think and talk like a Navajo.

All the same he could still turn on the roguish charm of his ancestors with an old friend, and that was how he greeted Ike Banner. The two of them gripped hands while Nathan undid the cinches of Ike's saddle harness and then assisted him to the ground.

The three seated themselves cross-legged inside Jack Lynch's hogan while his wife, who was Nathan's great-aunt, filled clay cups with *toghlepai* from a cork *tusjeh*. She sat placidly by, ready to pour refills, as they talked and sipped the powerful corn liquor. Thleen Chikeh understood hardly a word of her husband's native tongue, although she'd been his wife for over forty years.

"Well," said Jack Lynch after the usual exchange of pleasantries, "shall we out with it, Ike? Ye've come about the business of yesterday."

"I came to see an old friend, too."

"Aye, but you'll never need an excuse for that."

"I know. It's this damned arthritis. It holds a man down." Ike nodded his thanks to Thleen Chikeh as she refilled his cup. "Jack, how is the Hosteen boy doing?"

"Well enough, for one who's lost an eye and has gained not a few scars he'll carry to his grave." Jack Lynch pursed up his lips. "But the folks here were up in arms at what happened, I'll tell ye. I had to speak some fancy medicine to lay their tempers."

"I reckon it put you on a tough spot."

Jack Lynch smiled. "I'm used to being on the spot. It's bound to be touch-and-go for a white man who heads up a clan of the *Dineh*, even if he can shit blarney with the best of 'em. Further, as ye're well aware, a headman has no power as such, every Navajo bein' his own man. My part is but to advise and stand first in council. The only respect I'm accorded is that to which me gray hairs and sage words entitle me. . . ."

Nathan knew that the two old comrades would settle the matter without assistance from him, and he should be tending to the horses. He said so, and Jack Lynch nodded. "Go along, lad."

Nathan emptied his cup and handed it to his great-aunt, pressing her hand with a smile. Then he ducked out of the hogan, picked up the horses' trailing reins and tramped through the village toward a stream that bent around its far side.

As he swung along, Nathan's nose was pleasantly assailed by familiar smells: a greasy odor of cooking mutton, and the pungent one of sumac and piñon gum as he passed two women who were preparing a kettle of black dye over a low fire. He greeted them, and others he knew, and found most of their replies touched by the same barely polite reserve. To many of them, quite suddenly, Nathan Drew had become just another *Belinkana*—Navajo blood or not.

Not far from the stream bank, a man was sitting cross-legged under a brush arbor, working a crude bellows. In front of him was a pottery crucible set on a bed of glowing coals. Recognizing Adakhai, Nathan hesitated. Then he walked over to the arbor, leading the horses.

"*Ahalani, peshlikai*," said Nathan, greeting him with the Navajo term for silversmith.

Adakhai didn't trouble to glance up. "*Ha'at isha*?" he said harshly. "What do you want?"

"To ask after our cousin."

"Ask another place."

Had it been Adakhai who'd shot at them? Nathan wondered. He didn't think so. You could always be sure of one thing where Adakhai was concerned: the working of his fiery pride. He would stand up to a man, not take potshots at him from hiding.

"Banner himself has come to talk with Jack Lynch," Nathan said mildly. "The men who hurt Jimmy Hosteen no longer work for Banner."

Adakhai dropped a Mexican silver dollar into the crucible and pumped the cottonwood arms of the bellows, watching intently as the dollar began slowly to melt. Nathan watched too. He always found it curious that anyone of Adakhai's restless nature should choose to become versed in the patient, intricate craft of the *peshlikai*, but knew it was bound up with Adakhai's determination to preserve the old ways.

Nathan's anger of yesterday had cooled. The last thing he wanted was to feud with another Navajo. He could understand some of Adakhai's hot bitterness—even respect him in an obscure way. But Adakhai's deliberate ignoring of him was starting to nettle him all over. Nathan distrusted fanatics of any stripe. They were all rigidly dedicated, unbending to reason, and they were dangerous to have around.

" 'Lo there, Nate . . ."

The girl had come up quietly behind him, and now she spoke from a dozen feet away.

Nathan turned and looked at her with a mental shake of his head. Adakhai's half-sister was growing up, but she acted as much like a tough little kid as ever. A rather tall girl, she was as wiry as a cat. Her lean and wild look was enhanced by the man's rawhide leggings she wore with the usual blue velvet tunic of the Navajo woman. A belt of silver conches cinched it tight around her narrow waist. Her black hair was cropped short, like a white boy's, above her thin, pretty face.

Nathan said with a polite nod, "Hello, Lolly."

She faced him with a gamin grin, standing hipshot with a Winchester rifle in one hand, the other holding a straw on which she nibbled with strong white teeth. She tipped her head, pointing the straw at her brother.

"You won't get no satisfaction out of *him,*" she observed. "Wouldn't waste no time trying if I was you, Nate."

Adakhai glanced up at last, a black flame in his eyes. "You are a shame to the *Dineh,*" he snapped. "You ought to have your nose cut off."

Lolly grimaced and spat out the straw, laughing. "Hell, that old stuff only goes for married women who sleep around. Anyway, boy"—she hefted the rifle expertly—"you ever try it and I'll open you up like a can o' tomatoes."

"*Juth la hago ni!*" Adakhai spat. It was one of

the vilest of all Navajo epithets. The girl straightened up to her full height; a sting of blood flushed her brown skin.

Lolly had a temper like a wildcat, Nathan knew. To soften the tense moment, he gave her a smile and a wink, saying, "Was about to water these nags. Want to walk with me?"

The stain of warmth faded from the girl's cheeks; then she laughed. "Sure. Why not?"

She sauntered along at his side. They passed through an arm of scrubby cottonwoods and came to the willow-bordered stream. Nathan let the horses drink.

Lolly sank down on her haunches, gathered up a handful of pebbles and pitched them one by one at the water. Not looking at him, she said, "How's everything with you these days, Nate?"

"Same as ever, I reckon."

"Ever get into Cold River? To do a mite of hell-raising, I mean?"

Nathan smiled. "I figured you might mean that. I'm not much on raising hell, Lolly."

"No. You're a mighty proper man, Nate. As half-breeds go."

"Maybe that's why," Nathan said dryly. "A man who's half Indian doesn't just walk into a white man's town and set out to have himself a high old time. Not if he wants to keep his scalp, he doesn't. There's not two places in Cold River that would serve me a drink."

Lolly said idly, "Suppose not. How you manage at the whorehouses?"

Nathan felt a shock of heat in his face. He'd learned long ago not to judge Lolly Hosteen by the same standards he would judge any other woman, white or Indian. Once you accepted Lolly on her own terms, you were pretty well inured to anything she came up with. But she still caught him off-stride every now and then.

Noting the sly, puckish humor in her sidelong glance at him, he said coldly, "Could be your brother had a handy idea."

"Cut off my nose?"

"That. It's getting way out of joint."

Lolly laughed. She rose to her feet and dusted her hands off on her leggings. "Gee whillickers, Nate," she said innocently. "You really *are* proper. I mean, I know you're getting up in years and all, but you ain't *that* old. . . ."

"Maybe you better just shut your face for a spell."

She stuck out her tongue at him, then laughed again. "Yeah, maybe I had. Grandpa Jack always tells me I ain't respectful of my elders."

Nor much of anything else, Nathan thought sourly.

Lolly's full name was Lolita, and she was Mexican on her mother's side. Taken captive by the Navajo on some early-day raid, the mother had claimed mostly Spanish blood, and it came through strongly in the cast of Lolly's face, the narrow cheekbones and thin arch of her nose. But whatever her mixture of blood was, she was pure devil: spirited, fierce, wild-natured, raucous of tongue and defiant of any rules. She must be about sixteen now, and that was said to be kind of a dangerous age.

"What brings you and old Ike Banner here, Nate? I suppose it's what happened to Jimmy, huh?"

She spoke offhandedly, and the words didn't register with Nathan right away. He was gazing at the patch of red bandanna that showed at the throat of her tunic. The ends were tucked out of sight . . . but since when?

"Uh-huh," he murmured. "Say, is that a new rifle, Lolly? You care if I look it over?"

Nathan held out his hand as he spoke. Without thinking, she started to hand him the Winchester. Belatedly realizing or sensing what he had in mind, she tried to snatch it back. But Nathan's hand had already closed on the stock, and he gave a powerful sideward wrench. Lolly clung to the weapon, but swung helplessly with it. She lost her grasp and fell to her hands and knees.

Hissing a fierce curse, she sprang to her feet and leaped at him, both hands up, the fingers curved for his face. Nathan caught her right wrist, but her left-hand nails raked down the side of his face. He flung her roughly away, and this time she was slammed flat on her back.

She started to scramble up again. Nathan took a step forward and stood over her. "Don't do it again," he said thinly. "That was just pat-a-cake. Act like a hellion and you'll be treated like one."

Lolly stayed as she was, propped on her elbows and glaring up at him. Nathan opened the rifle's breech and sniffed it, grimacing at the reek of burned powder. He looked at the girl. "I would say this piece got some heavy use a little while back. What would you say?"

Lolly began to edge cautiously to her feet once more, and this time he let her get up. She batted at her dusty tunic, not meeting his eyes. "Can't a body practice with a new gun?"

"Practice, yes. But not on me or friends of mine."

"I don't know what you're talking about," she muttered.

"Ike and I got shot at, coming here. How did you know he was with me? You weren't around when we rode in."

"I was around, damn it! Use your damn eyes and you would of seen me!"

"Uh-huh. Where's that dun pony of yours? If he hasn't been ridden hard in the last hour, he won't be sweated, will he?"

Lolly sniffled and rubbed a palm across her nose. "All right." Her black eyes blazed at him. "I reckon you'll tell Grandpa Jack."

"First you tell me something. Why, Lolly? You weren't shooting to hit anyone . . . so what was it? All right, Jimmy is your cousin. He is mine too, in a shirttail way. But if you got the straight of things, you know I tried to help him. So why?"

"Oh for God's sake . . ." Again her gaze slipped away from his. "I was out looking for game and I seen you two coming. Thought I would have a little fun was all. What the hell, anyway!"

"Fun?" Nathan echoed. "You were having fun?"

"Yes, *fun*," she mimicked him sullenly. And held out her hand. "Just give it back now, will you?"

Nathan shook his head. "Don't reckon I'll take the chance. You had enough fun for one day."

Mouthing an oath, she came at him again. She tried to wrestle the rifle away, but Nathan was ready. He tossed the Winchester out of reach, wrapped his arms around Lolly and carried her struggling and kicking to the water's edge. He lifted strongly, thrusting her weight up and out before he let go of her.

Lolly hit the sluggish stream on her back. She let out a yip and sat up quickly. For a moment, sitting on the pebbly bottom in breast-deep water, she looked blank with surprise. Then she began to call him every name in the book, drawling them from between her teeth in a steady, monotonous way.

Nathan picked up the rifle and the horses' trailing reins, and headed back toward the village.

"You ain't so damn much, Nate Drew!" she yelled after him. "You think you're better'n any of us 'cause you live with them damn white people! Well, you ain't! You're just another damn breed to them. You . . . !" She paused on the brake of her own tearful rage. "I'll make you sorry! You wait and see if I don't!"

Nathan ground-hitched the horses in front of Jack Lynch's hogan. Entering, he seated himself on the bark mat in his former position and laid the Winchester at his feet. By now Jack Lynch and Ike were pretty mellow from the *toghlepai* and were exchanging equally mellow reminiscences. Apparently they had covered all the problems and had hashed out a rough agreement. Ike would tell him the details later on, Nathan knew.

Right now, he was uncomfortably aware of the scratches on his face and hoping that neither man would take any particular notice of them. Which Jack Lynch did, almost at once.

"Ah there, lad"—eyeing Nathan with a kind of shrewd benignity—"how did ye collect that pretty set o' clawmarks, eh? I've not been aware of any catamounts in this valley."

Nathan told of his encounter with Lolly, making it as brief and matter-of-fact as he could.

Jack Lynch picked up the rifle and sniffed the breech, and laid the weapon down with a grave nod.

"Well, that's Lolly for you." He held out his cup for Thleen Chikeh to refill. "Damn! There is no accounting for the acts of that girl. She has got a queer mixture of blood, and growing up in Lynchtown has brought out the wildest of it." He shook his head, chuckling. "Even when she wants a man to give her notice, she can think of no better way than to kick up the dust around him with a few bullets."

Ike, his eyes rheumy with the effects of corn liquor, leaned over and gave Jack Lynch a nudge. "You saying this here charming filly has got an eye on our friend here, Jack? Is that it?"

Jack Lynch nodded, still chuckling immoderately. "She's had it on him since she was a tyke. But the poor little wench don't know a way to show it save by shooting bullets close to him. *That* way, at least, she will finally get his notice, d'ye see?"

Nathan eyed him with a kind of shocked outrage, feeling the heat pour into his face.

He didn't believe a word of what Jack Lynch was saying. The old man's mind must be slipping from age and too much *toghlepai*. With an effort he curbed a surge of irritation and near-anger, saying tonelessly, "It's nothing to joke about, Jack. She is just a kid."

That brought an outbreak of guffaws from both his companions. Jack Lynch laughed almost silently, but Ike slapped his knee and roared. When he could manage to speak, Ike said, "Listen, son, there ain't no baby women. Just like there ain't no baby tigers."

"Well, I tell you . . ." Jack Lynch swirled the liquor in his cup. "It is nothing to laugh about when you get down to it. I have chided Lolly for her wild ways, but there is no controlling the girl. What's to do for her? Anywhere out o' Lynchtown, her lot would be all the worse. Her Indian blood would brand her." He shook his head. "Around here, though, all she does is get into devilment. Lately she has started to play hell with the young men. It may get to where I will have to fetch her a good larruping, which is no way to treat a growing girl."

Nathan still felt a warmth of embarrassment, and he was relieved when the talk swung back to the matter that had brought them here. Jack Lynch thought that Ike's firing of the Purley clan would head off any trouble here in Lynchtown.

"What about the likes of this young Adakhai?" Ike asked. "That's all that worries me. Can you hold any hotbloods like him in rein?"

Jack Lynch shrugged his shaggy brows. "I think so. Adakhai's bark is fiercer than his bite. I've given him a talking to, never fear. Don't forget, he is the son of my oldest daughter. No matter what he comes out and says, he has the respect for me that's due a grandsire. But I'm bound to say it again, Ike . . . I've mistrustings about the intentions of that oldest boy of yours."

"Don't worry about Thorp," Ike said grimly. "He won't take a damn thing away from you people, no matter what happens to me."

"I know." Jack Lynch nodded. "It's only that I wish there was no black feelings between your blood and mine."

Nathan glanced from one of them to the other, feeling another wash of irritation. They were talking around him now. How—if something did happen to Ike—could anyone guarantee what Thorp Banner would or wouldn't do? Plainly, the two old men knew something he didn't. Just as plainly, they had no intention of saying out loud what it was.

But why?

CHAPTER 8

Even with the door and several small windows open, the bunkhouse was like an oven. The heat had climbed through the day, and early darkness had not relieved it. Heat seemed to drench the bunkroom like a torrid vapor, mingling with the odors of sweat and tobacco smoke.

Four of the six men playing poker at the scarred table in the room's center were Swallowtail punchers. The other two were Nathan Drew and Tyrone Banner.

Ty was about as drunk as Nathan had ever seen him. He had lost steadily through the evening and couldn't have cared less, even if the table stakes hadn't been penny ante. It was a wonder he could still hold a fan of cards in his fist, much less follow the play.

Finally his head and shoulders pitched forward on the table; he passed out. Nathan pushed back his chair and hoisted Ty's limp form half upright.

"Need any help, Nate?" a puncher asked.

Nathan shook his head. "Thanks, Tom. Good night." He ducked his head and let Ty collapse across his shoulders. Then he walked slowly out of the bunkhouse, aware of the low mutters of the crew behind him, and headed for the house.

A wind was combing the night in short hard gusts, rattling the leaves of cottonwoods that flanked the big house. Thunder reverberated gently in the west. Rain soon. That would break the heat. But it still hung like damp layers of wool as Nathan tramped up the long slope to the house, perspiring heavily under Ty's dead weight.

This was an old story to him. He had packed Ty home dead drunk from Cold River after more than one night of carousing. It was part of friendship's duty that he took on phlegmatically and never thought much about. All the same, he took a dim view of Ty taking on a load and then intruding on a friendly game in the bunkhouse. The players couldn't refuse to let the boss's son sit in, but it made for a hell of a bad example.

If Ty wanted to drink himself to death, it was his business. When his behavior began to undercut Swallowtail's pride and morale, a lot more was involved.

The wind was picking up, blowing steadily now as Nathan paused under a cottonwood and eased his burden to the ground. Sweat was pouring off him; he needed to rest for a minute.

He wouldn't take Ty into the house by the front door, of course. This early in the evening, Ike would still be up, reading, in his parlor. Luckily each room in the house's sleeping area—a long wing that was attached to the east side of the low, rambling main house—had a door that opened on the outside as well as one fronting on the bedroom corridor. That had been a shrewd provision of Ike's when he'd built the wing many years ago, reckoning that with three sons, he would have to make allowance for their skylarking when they came of age. Equipping their rooms with outside doors would enable them to slip in after hours without rousing the household. All three had made good use of this convenience over the years.

Nathan supposed that Serena would be lying sleepless in her bed. Waiting for her errant spouse to stumble in or be carried in. How many nights had she spent in this way?

Only Serena knew, and she would never say. Out of loyalty or timidity, she never condemned Ty's actions to others. And maybe not to Ty himself. If Ty was a hopeless case, maybe so was his wife, for tolerating his behavior. *Look who's talking!* Nathan thought wryly. But his part was small enough. All he had to do was carry Ty to the door, tap on it to bring Serena, help her put Ty to bed and take his leave. Simple.

Thunder was rolling out of the west in deepening waves. Tongues of lightning flickered, lending the yard a fitful illuminance. Wind swelled to crescendo as it roared through the cottonwoods, whipping and tossing them in a fury. Nathan hoisted Ty to his shoulders again and walked on. He sidled up to the outer door of Ty and Serena's room and raised his hand to knock.

The faint noises from inside stopped him. It was hard to make them out above the blast of wind. The single window by the door was dark. What in hell was going on in there?

Nathan dumped Ty on the patio flags and pressed his ear to the doorboards. Then he knew.

Thorp Banner's voice: hoarse, gutteral, ugly. And Serena's, giving out little muffled screams.

Nathan pushed on the door. It was unbarred and unlatched. It swung inward with a faint creak of hinges.

A flare of lightning filled the room. Its illumination lasted only an instant, but it showed all there was to be seen. Thorp had Serena pinned across the bed. Her nightgown was torn almost away, and Thorp's big hand was clamped over her mouth, stifling her cries to frenzied whimpers. His left arm was beneath her circling her waist, arching her body to him in a crushing embrace.

In the moment before the white dazzle of light passed, Thorp's face swung toward Nathan. The eyes wore a crazed sheen; his teeth were bared like an animal's. *Drunk!* thought Nathan.

He stepped into the room just as Thorp whipped up and around to face him. Instinctively, Nathan took a long step sideways in the dark. He felt the solid punch that Thorp threw at his head fan past his ear. Nathan grappled him; they wrestled around the room.

Thorp was drunk as a skunk, but even addled with booze, he was still a powerhouse of sheer bone and muscle. Nathan kept straining away from the full clasp of his burly arms. Built like a young bull himself, he was nearly a head shorter than Thorp and lacked a good forty pounds of his beef. If Thorp ever got those great arms around him, he would have an unbreakable hold; he might even crack a man's ribs.

Nathan managed to wedge a forearm under Thorp's shelving chin. Slowly, putting out all his strength, he shoved Thorp's head backward to a painful angle.

At last, with a grunting curse, Thorp let go his hold on Nathan and stumbled back a step, barely catching his balance. In that instant, Nathan bent, wrapped his arms around Thorp's massive thighs—and lifted. His muscles cracked as he heaved Thorp up and clear of the floor.

The window was at Thorp's back; his over-balanced torso swayed toward it. Nathan thrust with the direction of Thorp's leaning and then he let go. Thorp's bulk crashed against the window and through it, taking panes of glass and part of the weathered sash with it. As he went through, the sill caught him behind the knees and flipped him over. Thorp hit the stone-flagged patio in a shower of shattered glass.

Nathan turned to Serena as lightning flared again. It showed her sitting bolt upright in bed, eyes wild with terror, hands pressed to her bleeding mouth. She was all right for the moment, and Nathan wheeled and went out the open door.

The shuttling flicker of skyfire washed constantly over the patio as Thorp crawled dazedly to his hands and knees. He shook his head like a ringy bull, then tipped up his face. It was laced by a bloody darkness of streaming cuts.

"You goddamn fucking breed. I'll kill you for that."

The words seemed dredged out of a vast weariness. Thorp could barely manage to stagger to his feet now. Then he swayed violently, unable to quite straighten up. Nathan took two steps, bringing his hand back. He landed one hard, flat, contemptuous slap that swiveled Thorp's head with it. That was all it took.

Thorp toppled backward, his head rapping solidly on the flagstones. He lay still. Then he groaned, loud and long.

Nathan moved back to the open doorway. "Mrs. Banner?"

"Y—yes . . ."

"Your brother-in-law is just about out cold. He'll be all right. Put a blanket or something around yourself, will you?"

There were rustling sounds in the dark, and then Serena said, "All right."

Nathan entered the room and stepped to his

right till he touched the commode, on whose marble top he knew that a big lamp rested. He struck a match and lighted the lamp, and turned the wick low as the feeble saffron light spread through the room. Serena stood by the bed, wearing a plum-colored robe of some silky material. She was pressing a handkerchief to her cut lip, and her face still held a sickness of terror that wasn't pleasant to see.

Nathan walked back to Ty, bent over and caught him by the wrists and hauled him up, then carried him inside to the bed. "He's drunk is all," he said tersely.

Serena didn't reply. Mechanically, she crossed unsteadily to the wash stand, poured some water with shaking hands, dipped her handkerchief and dabbed at her lip. "Oh God," she whispered. "Oh God!"

"How did it happen?"

"I . . . was lying in the dark, awake. I heard a knock at the outside door and I . . . I thought it must be you, bringing Tyrone home. I got up and slipped the latch and . . . *he* came in. Just like that. And he seized me. Oh God!"

She was shuddering violently now, and she bent her face against the handkerchief and began to cry. "I . . . I . . . I don't know what to do! He was drunk, wasn't he?"

"Pretty drunk," said Nathan. "But that's no excuse. Ike should be told about this."

"No!" Serena said it vehemently, swiftly turning to face him. "No, Mr. Drew—please. I don't want any more trouble . . . we've had so much already. Too much!"

Nathan eyed her with a cool patience. "Ma'am, I have seen how Thorp looks at you. I never reckoned he would pull a stunt like this. But I should have remembered when he goes on a bat, he goes crazy. If he—"

"Can't it be managed?" Her voice trembled on the edge of hysteria. "The wind and thunder must have covered any noise . . . and I can say the window got broken by accident. Can't I do that?"

"Well, I suppose so, sure. But I was about to say, if he did something like this once, he could have it in him to do it again."

He might as well talk against the wind, Nathan saw. The wild and unreasoning fear that Serena felt lay naked in her face. She was terrified of Thorp Banner. He realized, even before she spoke, that her shocked mind held only one thought: not to antagonize Thorp any further.

"No . . . no, I beg of you. Mr. Banner must not hear of this. Nor must Ty, ever. You mustn't tell either of them. Please!"

Nathan suppressed the surge of pitying disgust he felt. He nodded once, curtly. "Can you take care of your husband now?"

"Yes . . . yes."

"All right. And Mrs. Banner—" Nathan had

turned to the door and he halted there, his hand on the latch. "You bar this door after I go out and keep it that way hereafter. Especially if you're alone. Same for the inside door. Is there a lock on it?"

She nodded mutely.

"You don't ever open either of them to anyone till he's identified himself," Nathan said flatly. "Understand?"

Not waiting for her answer, he walked out and shut the door behind him. He paused till he heard the swingbar drop into place behind it, then moved over to Thorp, who still lay groaning on the patio. Rain had started to fall, its chill wetness plastering Nathan's shirt to his back. In the blaze of lightning, he watched rain lave Thorp's face and slowly mat his hair.

"Goddamn you, breed," he husked. Staring up at Nathan, his eyes seemed livid with blue fire. "You gonna pay the piper, boy. I am gonna break you into more pieces than anyone will care to pick up. I swear it to you."

"You just lay there and cool off a spell," Nathan told him. "Nothing like a cold shower to settle a body's humors. Sober him up, too. You got luckier than you know, Thorp."

CHAPTER 9

I tell you it's them goddamn Navajos," insisted Thorp.

Slacked in his swivel chair with hands folded across his belly, Ike Banner eyed his eldest son with a weary disgust. Thorp leaned with folded arms in the doorway of Ike's office. Big and arrogant and jut-jawed, he dominated the small, cluttered room.

"I don't give a damn for your unfounded opinions," said Ike. "I told you—"

"Yeah, yeah. I know. Jack Lynch sent a man to tell you his Injuns spotted signs of rustling on our top range. So what? That's a handmade cover story if I ever heard one."

Ike's brows drew down. "Jack Lynch is the best friend I got alive," he said quietly. "You don't call him a liar. Not to my face. Not ever. You hear?"

Thorp grimaced, then winced a little. He had gotten a number of deep cuts on his head and neck a week back and they were just half-healed. He hadn't said how it happened and Ike hadn't asked, figuring it was just the result of another drunken bat. Thorp still looked like someone had dumped him through a window or something.

"Sure, I know. Old Jack is the prince of shamrocks. Only granting that's so, what'd keep them bucks o' his from fancying up a lie to the old man? Goddammit, Pa, I have cut the sign for myself. Jags of our beef been trailed off over our northwest line by riders. They had barefoot horses, and that's Injun."

"Trailed *where,* dammit?" Ike thumped a fist on his rolltop desk. "You follow any sign to Lynchtown?"

"Christ, no. I never said them red niggers was dumb, did I? They would have the smarts to move stolen beef away from their own stamping grounds."

"Then push branded cattle across the mountains and try to peddle 'em in, say, Caldwell?" Ike said dryly. "Huh-uh. If they tried it without showing a bill of sale from the owner, the Cattlemen's Association would get word of it to me."

"Who said aught about selling? They would do what I told you they been doing for years. Slaughtering our cows for their own use. But by God, you can't write off this kind o' plain-out steal as winterloss, Pa!"

Ike painfully stretched his legs, eyeing the toe of his boot. "Never said I could. What about that Purley tribe, now?"

He glanced up to catch a veiled narrowing of Thorp's look.

"What about 'em, Pa? I sent 'em packing like you said. Out of our line camp and off our land."

Ike nodded musingly. "I wonder how far they got."

Thorp glowered. "What was it you said about *my* unfounded opinions?"

"You say Sixto Larraldes brought you the word about the rustling sign this morning?"

"That's right, Pa. I put him and Pinky Miller on the line-camp duty after I give them Purleys the boot. They're good men, the both."

"Ain't disputing it."

Ike barely knew those two crewmen; he'd little more than a brushing acquaintance with Swallowtail's recently acquired hands. That was a province he'd allotted to Thorp, and he was determined not to interfere with it.

"I suppose," said Ike, "your man Larraldes didn't try to follow up that sign?"

"Said he lost it a ways into the foothills."

Ike gave another slow, musing nod. "What I think I'll do is ride up that way myself and have a look around."

"Yeah?" Thorp didn't trouble to keep the sardonic amusement from his voice. "Better take your pet breed along. He can pack your carcass back."

"Damn you!" A flare of unexpected temper brought Ike half out of his chair, gripping the arms. "Don't smart-mouth me, boy! I can still get on a horse and off him by myself if I got to. I still got eyes in my head and a brain in my skull, and

126

there's naught gone wrong with either. Don't you forget it!"

"Fancy me doing that," Thorp said lazily. "Hell, Pa, I know you're still 'bout as spry as old Satan. Takes some good bending-over muscle to kiss all them Injun asses good and proper."

Ike heaved to his feet, his face swelling with angry blood, and Thorp backed away, holding his hands palms out. He said with a good-natured chortle, "Hold it, Pa. Jesus, I'm just joking! Don't get your pecker up. And I lay odds you still can, huh?"

Ike halted, fisting and unfisting his hands. "I can still kick ass, too, even if it hurts like hell. So get the bejasus out of here before I make us both sorry. All right?"

Thorp backed out of the room, grinning and bowing. He gave another hoot of laughter as he banged out the front door.

Seething, Ike settled back in his chair. Damn the insufferable insolence of that whelp! After a moment his mouth relaxed in a dour grin. He was used to the ways of rough-and-rowdy men, and he'd sired a prime specimen in Thorp. But Thorp went too damned far. Or at least to the far edge of what he could safely get away with, and that wore a man fine . . .

Was Thorp right? Had he gone too damned old or too damned soft? Ike sat fiercely denying it. Once in a while the question gnawed at him a little. But now in his anger, it bit like an angry tooth.

Old? Maybe. Soft? *Like hell!*

Again he heaved upright, clumped out to the parlor and got his coat and hat, then slammed out the door.

Serena looked up, startled. She was on her knees by the veranda, trimming the Prairie Queen rosebushes that Luella had planted so long ago. For a moment, surprised by the sight of her as he'd often seen Luella when she was looking after her beloved roses, Ike pulled up short.

"How's the flowers, lass?"

"They're fine." Serena smiled nervously. "You don't mind, do you, sir? I know Mrs. Banner loved these bushes, Ty said so. . . ."

"Lord, no. Tend 'em all you like."

Ike's words came more gruffly than he'd intended, and he tramped heavily on toward the corral. After years of coping with Lu's gentle iron, he was embarrassed by Serena's timid ways. *Women!* Lu had always baffled him, and for a different reason, so did Serena.

Luella. So many little signs of her, reminders of what she had been in his life, lingered around the place, ghostlike and yet tangible. Memory stabbed him with a bitter force and raked up the coals of his anger all over.

A lot of dust was kicking up in the breaking

corral as Sandal Cruz tried to ride the kinks out of a balky bronc.

Nate Drew had finally yielded to Sandal's pleas and was introducing him to the lore of horsebreaking, but a little at a time. Each day he let Sandal ride the rough edges off a horse, one already broken but still fractious, and always under Nathan's supervision. Old Diego was there too, and so was Ty.

Just now Ty's sketchbook and pencil were idle in his hands. He was caught up in a mild excitement, watching the contest, and suddenly he yelled, "That's it, kid! Stick him out! Ride him high and low!"

Nathan shook his head. "He's not ready for this one yet." He raised his voice. "Get off him, *nino*! Take a dive!"

Obediently Sandal tipped out of the saddle, landed in the horsebreaker's roll and scrambled out between the fence poles. He was dusty and grinning.

Nathan smiled at Diego. "He's coming along."

Diego Cruz shrugged, carefully masking his pride. *"Poco á poco."*

Ty, as if ashamed of his brief exuberance, dug a flask out of his pocket, uncapped it and took a long pull.

It was one more nettle in Ike's craw. He wouldn't comb Ty over in front of ranch help, but for a moment it took all his willpower not to.

Christ! Why had he permitted Ty to run himself to seed this way? It had to stop, by God. It was going to stop.

Soft! Maybe I been that, all right. No more!

"Don't stand there with your teeth hanging out," he said harshly to Sandal. "Fetch my rig and cinch it on Blackie."

"Sure, *patrón!*"

Nathan said, "Going for a ride?"

"No, for a stroll on the heather," bristled Ike. "What the hell's it look like?"

"Like you're going for a ride. Want some company?"

"No, dammit! Can't a man get on a goddamn horse without flushing out a Navajo nursemaid?"

"Whatever you say."

Ike hoisted himself into the saddle with some effort and pain, and nobody offered to help. Clumsily he fastened the buckles of the harness himself, aware that they were all careful not to look at him and were wondering at his temper. And he was damned if he was going to apologize.

He rode away from Swallowtail headquarters in a direction that was roughly north and east. Moving steadily through the golden, windy morning, he felt some of his anger lift. *Jesus,* he thought, *you're getting spookier than a cur at ticktime. Take it easy.* But anger left its obstinate residue in his mouth, and he was damned if he was going to let it all go.

130

Thorp needed taking down a peg. Ty needed bracing up. And Free, who was a half-formed replica of Thorp, with all Thorp's damned lollygagging ways and little of his strength or sense, needed to be taken in hand and damned soon.

I'll get to it, Ike promised himself.

The sun was high, beating hot against his back, as the terrain began to change. Too damned hot to ride this far and then advance into the rugged foothills. Awkwardly Ike peeled off his coat and fastened it to his cantle. The weight of his years plucked at his muscles; a steady ache spread through his body.

He'd noticed the same seeping weariness on that ride with Nate Drew last week. It was a thing he could barely admit to himself, much less to another man.

Jack Lynch's Navajo messenger had given him a fair idea of where to look for rustlers' sign. Along the east bank of the Pelado River where it snaked across the mountains, the Pelado ran both wide and shallow for miles of its lower course, and it looked as if the cow-lifters had used water to cover their track. They could drive the stolen animals a long way upstream and then leave the water on any shelf of bare rock where it sloped to the bank. They'd have rugged going across the peaks, but just a few patient men working small bunches of cows could manage it.

Ike saw the sparkle of the river through a motte of cottonwoods ahead, and now he swerved to parallel the river course while he slowly scanned the ground. He was so intent on looking for track that he failed to see the two horsemen emerging from the line of trees off to his right.

Not till one of them said loudly, "Hey-ey, Sheb! Look at that there, now. It is that ole booger tole us to get offa his land!"

The Purley brothers gigged their horses forward at a leisurely gait.

Ike quartered his mount around just enough to face them. His eyes narrowed; his jaw hardened. He wasn't afraid of their stripe of scum, but right now he wished he had a rifle ready to hand. A Winchester was sheathed under his leg, but the Purleys were packing sidearms, and they were already too close for him to risk pulling long iron on them.

Claud and Sheb Purley pulled up in front of him, taking their time as they urged their horses a little apart, sidling off somewhat to the right and left of him. They were both red-faced and sweating, and it wasn't all from the heat. Ike knew a whiskey flush when he saw one.

"I'm trailing up cow thieves," he said flatly. "Maybe you men can help me out."

"Well, for shit's sake!" Claud declared. "Fancy that. You hear him, Sheb? Cow thieves." He leaned forward and crossed his arms on his pommel, sort of leering. "Aw right, Grampaw. You say how we mought be of use. Speak right up."

"You might of seen something going on. Cut sign on 'em, even. Seeing you are still hanging near onto my land."

"Yeah," Claud murmured. "Ever sincet you had us throwed off it. Well, we ain't on it now. You have rode across your own north line, and we are all on free range."

Ike shrugged. "Could be."

He didn't like the situation: not the way the two were casually edging their mounts nearer on either side of him, nor the wicked relish that colored Claud's tone. No telling anything from the whiskey-varnished blankness of Sheb's stare. So Ike barely watched Sheb, and that was a mistake.

As Ike's gaze shifted fully to Claud, he felt rather than saw the sudden movement to his right. And spun to grab at his saddle gun. Too late. Sheb leaned out and yanked the Winchester free of its scabbard and reined back, all in one motion. Without looking at the rifle he sent it sailing over his shoulder.

Ike's horse was prancing nervously. He held the gelding on a tight rein and said between his teeth, "You go pick that up and hand it back and we'll just forget this happened. All right?"

"Grampaw," said Claud, "we don't take naught

off you no more. Not a lick of it. That there includes orders."

All the submerged meanness in Claud Purley was welling to the surface, fed by enough liquor to carry him past caution. It made his face pure-quill ugly. Ike didn't know what the brothers had in mind for him, and he wasn't about to allow them time to show him.

His only chance was to move fast. And move at once.

He let out a stentorian yell and cracked his heels into Blackie's flanks with all the force he could muster. Red pain shot up his weakened legs, almost cutting the yell in half.

The black lunged forward between the Purleys and bolted across the open meadow toward the fringe of forest. Ike's whole body was battered by arthritic agony; it slid in waves across his brain, almost blotting out thought and sensation.

He tried to turn Blackie south, back toward the Swallowtail line. But in the crush of pain he could only slump across the horse's mane, held to its back by his saddle harness while he was jolted up and down like a sack of meal.

Ike retained enough presence of mind to grasp the reins and fight for control of his mount. But it was useless.

He was dimly aware of the Purley brothers whooping in drunken glee as they raced their horses along either side of him, whipping at

Blackie's rump with their fist-doubled hats. Ordinarily the gentlest of mounts, the black was goaded to a near-frenzy by this treatment. He lengthened his stride to a leg-stretching run that quickly left the Purleys behind.

The two brothers pulled up and sat their horses, laughing.

The panicked black burst into a thicket of chokecherry brush and crashed through it, and hit another stretch of open meadow.

Christ, I can't stop him! Got to get off . . .

Ike was nearly unconscious, but that dim thought pushed through his crumbling senses. Somehow he fumbled out his pocket knife and got the large blade open.

A slash of razor-edged steel. Then another. Fumbling for each harness strap and sliding the blade beneath each one, then twisting the knife upward. Two straps parted. Now the third—

Ike had to work fast, clinging desperately to the black's mane as he made the cuts. All four straps must be cut, both his feet freed of the stirrups, before he left the saddle.

Otherwise he would be dragged to his death.

The fourth strap parted.

With his last strength, Ike pitched sideways and outward, his body voluntarily relaxing to the loose rolling fall that a lifetime of straddling spirited horseflesh had ingrained in him.

The impact as he hit the ground seemed little

more than a numb blow. And then he kept rolling, his body slack, to lessen his impetus.

The last thing Ike remembered was the mossy boulder that he was hurtling toward, his body rolling over and over toward it. *No way of stopping!* His head collided with the rock.

And everything was wiped out.

Snake Purley was scouting upstream a ways to see if he could flush a rabbit or two for the stew-pot. Claud and Sheb had hankered to hunt along the lower reaches of the river.

It was the faint drift of Ike's yell that brought Snake downstream on the run, heeling his pinto horse for speed.

For Snake, his reaction was almost a reflex. If some kind of fooferaw was going on down that way, Snake didn't have to ask, he could almost be sure, sight unseen, that his crackbrained boys were somehow involved.

Snake burst out of the trees and rode fast across a broad meadow. He saw deep-dug prints in the turf, sign of running horses, and tailed them up fast. He burst through a growth of chokecherry brush.

He was ready for almost anything, but what he found was so disastrous that, on his first sight of it, Snake's mind went blank. There were the two clabber-headed bastards he'd sired sitting their horses and wearing dumb-faced looks. And there was Ike Banner on the ground, folded against a big rock and lying very still.

Feeling queasy at the pit of his stomach, Snake swung off his mount and hurried to Ike's side. He was lying face up, blood trickling through his white hair and down his temple. His head rested against the rock.

"Jesus God," Snake murmured.

He felt for a heartbeat and found it. His first reaction was one of surging relief. It raveled away quickly.

Rising off his haunches, Snake tramped over to his sons and squinted up at them. "Get down," he said flatly.

Claud and Sheb slowly dismounted, not meeting their father's eyes.

"Now, you dumb bastards. Just suppose you say what happent here. Speak up, Claud!"

Claud stumbled out the gist of what had happened, prodded along by a few stinging queries from his pa.

Snake fixed both his sons with his pale-wicked stare. He even lifted off the whip coiled around his neck. But then he only fingered it for a goodly while, eyeing his sons with a chill disgust.

"Aw right," he said at last. "What's done's done. But God, if you ain't the dumbest sons a bitches I seen in my born days. You know what this means? You got that much brains?"

Claud blinked uncertainly. "All we had in mind was to hooraw the ole fart a little bit, Pappy."

Sheb merely blinked.

Snake stared at his sons. "Jesus! Well, what it means, you dung-brain whipoorwhills, is that we are left with no choice. None a-tall. That ole man is still alive. But we can't leave him that way."

A slow understanding filtered into Claud's broad red face. "Oh, yeh. I see, Pappy. You mean our asses could get in a real cinch when Mr. Ike Banner tells what has happent to him."

"Claud, you must of been eating razor soup, you are that sharp," Snake said softly. "On account of hoorawing Mr. Ike Banner and bunging him up, we mought just get hunted down by a sheriff's posse. We would all of us get calaboosed for a goodly time for sure. Also, if there was a posse on the hunt for us, they would stand a goodly chance of uncovering the job we done of thieving Mr. Banner's cattle. And that would get us calaboosed two, three times as long."

Snake paused. "So even you two got to see what we have got to do now. And it has got to look like an accident."

CHAPTER 10

In a stand of pine in back of one of the barns, Thorp Banner was practicing with an oversize bullwhip. He'd lined up a row of tin cans on a deadfall and, standing a full whip's length away, was snapping them off one at a time with a deadly force and accuracy.

He smiled and coiled his whip. Not a single miss. He walked over to the deadfall and set the cans up again.

From behind him his brother Free said idly, "Boo," and laughed when it brought Thorp whirling around.

Thorp scowled and walked over to him. "You don't go prowling up back of a man that way, kid. It could get you dead damned quick."

"What'll you get me dead with, that thing?"

Thorp raised a huge fist with the coiled whip in it. "You think I couldn't, sonny boy? I could take your head half off with it, was I minded."

Free laughed again. Suddenly he brought his right-hand Colt blurring from its holster. He fired five times in rapid succession, and with each shot a can went bounding off the deadfall. Afterward he pushed the spent loads out of his pistol, grinning.

"There's your answer, big bro," he said. "You couldn't bring it into action near fast enough. A good pistolman 'ud have you leaking five places 'fore you could pull your whip arm back."

Thorp showed his big teeth, smiling. "Well, that is real impressive, baby brother. I never claimed to be no shakes with a hogleg, but you best not get thinking a lot of flashy gunplay is all you need to club the wolf away from the door. You could still get dead before you know it. Even a greenhorn with a few smarts under his hat could hang up your spurs for you."

"Like hell!" laughed Free. "How?"

A startled look crossed Thorp's face.

Free said sharply, "What the hell is it?" And quickly turned his head, following his brother's glance. An instant later, he felt something hard jam into his side below the ribs.

Free grunted and looked down. The hard object was the butt of Thorp's whipstock.

Thorp said with his great horsey grin, "That's how. Jesus, kid"—shaking his head in wonderment—"it's just like old man Barnum said. There's one like you born every minute."

Free flushed with anger, but Thorp chuckled and clapped him on the shoulder. "Don't get your risibles up, now. Having a swelled head is what has always got your ass in a crack. Freeman, if you ever got thinking you're about a quarter as good as you think you are, you might get to be twice as good as you think you are."

"Which would make me about half as good as you, I suppose," Free said sourly.

Thorp roared out his mirth. "See? You're getting some smarts already!"

Free began to reload his Colt, eyeing the whip curiously. "Ain't seen you break that thing out since I was a tad. How come now?"

"Just for the hell of it. Thought I might be a mite rusty with it."

"I can remember how you used to pop a fly off a mule's ass with it."

"Did I? Well, I got to get my arm back. It will take a spell."

The two strolled out of the grove and back around the barn. Late afternoon shadows stretched across the yard; banners of early sunset streaked the western sky.

"Wonder where the old man is?" said Free. "Hadn't he ought to be back by now?"

Thorp shrugged. "Long ride to our north line and just as long a ride back. Hell, he got on the peck at me, and I reckon he had to ride it out of his system. There's still a couple hours of daylight."

"Yeah." After a brief silence Free added, "Thought I might mosey into town tonight."

"Wondered why you was all gussied up like a French pimp. You wouldn't have yourself something that's sweet and randy waiting for you, now would you?"

Free grinned, a little smugly. "Whatever give you that idea?"

In contrast to Thorp's habits, he disliked being unkempt, always bathing and sprucing up after a day on-range. Whenever he went to town, Free went in his spanking-best duds. Right now he wore range clothes, but with a new calf-hide vest and flowered sleeve garters over a red-and-white-striped shirt. For added show, he wore a pair of ivory-handled pistols cross-belted at his narrow hips.

Thorp slowly nodded, grinning too. "All right, hotshot. You go 'long and have all the fun you want. Just keep your damn nose clean for once, all right?"

"Come on, Thorp . . . I don't raise no more hell than you."

"Sure I raise hell. But I cover my tracks and you don't."

"What of it?"

"I tell you what of it. The old man has gone on the peck at me over and over about all the damn shenanigans you pull. He expects me to keep you in line. I don't fancy the job any, but . . ."

"Yeah? Think you could do that?"

Thorp's face hardened; Free winced at the sudden bite of iron fingers on his arm.

"Don't get your pecker up with me, sonny," Thorp said gently. "All you got is just about enough to pee with. You kick up any more dust that settles under the old man's nose, and I am going to do some good hard ass-kicking. You believe it, hear?"

"All right. Christ, Thorp!"

But now Thorp's gaze was moving past Free, across the yard toward a horseman who was coming into sight from beyond the corrals. He was leading another horse with something bulky slung across its back.

"That's Sixto Larraldes," Thorp muttered. "Now what's he . . . ?"

A sharp, premonitory feeling made a coldness in Thorp's belly. Without more words now, he went swiftly forward to meet Larraldes, and Free was at his heels.

In a few seconds more they had the answer. Ike Banner was slung motionless across his saddle. His clothing was wet and he was colorless and limp.

"*Muerto*," Larraldes said softly. "I am sorry."

"Pappy," whispered Free. "God, Thorp . . ."

But Thorp's pale gaze was already impaling Larraldes. "What happened, Sixto?"

Larraldes shook his head. He was a scarred, stocky man in his mid-thirties. "That is the question. I ain' sure. But I'm tell you what we find. A few hours ago Pinky Miller an' me are working out from the line camp, west toward the Pelado. We see this horse standing free over by the bank, an' we go have a look. Then we find

Mr. Banner. He is lay face down in the water."

Thorp fingered an end of one slashed harness strap on Ike's saddle. "This here was cut with a knife. How you explain that?"

"*Quién sabe*? It look to us like maybe this black horse, he run away with you pa. So you pa cut the straps to get off him. But by now they have reach the river, it very shallow there, an' your pa fall in the water. Is hit his head, we think. There is a mark by his ear. An' so he is knock' out an' face down in the water. So, we think, he drown."

Free said in a stunned voice, "But this Blackie horse, he is as gentle a thing as ever was. That's why Pappy rode him. I mean, would he go on the spook that bad? So bad Pappy couldn't hold him in?"

"Maybe," said Larraldes. "A rattlesnake can do that to a horse. The horse, he go out of his head."

Thorp parted the white hair of Ike's temple to examine the great bruise on his scalp. Ike's knife was missing, he noted, but his saddle gun was in its scabbard.

Nodding slowly, Thorp said, "I reckon it could of happened that way, Sixto. Pretty near that way."

After the supper hour Thorp spoke to the assembled crew in the bunkhouse, telling them of Ike's death. For the time being, he told them, the ranch routine would continue as usual. Maybe there would be some changes later on. The crew would have tomorrow off for the funeral.

That done, he and Free went back to the main house, walking slowly through the darkness to clear the fumes of whiskey from their heads. Both felt the residues of a shock they had attempted to blunt by killing a quart of whiskey. They had drunk for several hours, but it was like drinking ice water except for dulling their senses a little.

You couldn't wipe the death of a man like Ike Banner out of mind with mere booze. Neither son, maybe, was quite sure what he'd felt for the old man. But that he'd been an overwhelming force in their lives couldn't be denied.

They entered the house by way of the kitchen, where Serena and Celestina were cleaning up the remnants of a supper hardly anyone had touched. Barging through the door, Thorp nearly collided with Serena, whose nerves were drawn so fine that she dropped a cup, breaking it. Then she stood stock-still and just stared at him, fear gliding behind her face.

For once Thorp didn't trouble to bait her. He gave her a stony abstracted look, then stepped around her and passed through the house, followed by Free, to Ike's office at the rear.

Thorp felt for and lighted the big lamp

suspended by a wire from the ceiling. As sallow light flickered through the room, he glanced at Free who stood uncertainly in the doorway, blinking.

"Either go sleep it off," Thorp said irritably, "or come in and shut the damn door."

"What you aim to do?"

"Find the old man's will." Thorp was already rummaging through the battered rolltop desk. "You hear what I said?"

Free stepped into the room and closed the door. "Uh, maybe we oughta wait till after the funeral? I mean . . ."

"Wait, hell," Thorp declared almost savagely. "I waited long enough already!" Then he said more quietly, "The old man has joined the majority, kid. Won't make no difference to him. We got interests of our own to look after. Meaning how he has left us fixed. I don't see no odds in waiting till his lawyer, old Haberstrom, calls us to a reading of the will. I know the old man kept a copy of his own, and more'n likely it's in his safe. I bust the damn thing open if I got to, but maybe . . ."

Going through the litter of a bottom drawer of the desk, Thorp turned up a faded slip of paper that must have been stowed there long ago. The numbers and letters penciled on it were almost illegible. He held it up to the light, squinting.

"Yeah, this is it. Combination to the safe."

Free cleared his throat. "Maybe ole Tyrone oughta be in on this, if we're gonna—"

"Hell," Thorp cut in roughly. "The load that silly bastard took on after I told him about the old man, he'll be dead to the world till noon tomorrow."

He squatted in front of the small iron safe that had occupied a corner of Ike's cramped office for as long as he could remember. After fooling with the dial for several minutes, swearing as his big crooked fingers fumbled the combination twice, Thorp felt the tumblers click into place. He turned the handle and swung open the door.

He swept just a cursory glance over the safe's contents. All this stuff would have to be gone through, but in good time. Just now his interest lay in a small tin box where he knew Ike kept his most important papers. Thorp lifted it out and opened it, rifling quickly through till he found the copy of his father's will whose stipulations Ike had casually described to him several years ago.

Thorp scanned it with an "Ah!" of satisfaction. As expected, the holograph document, written in Ike's own (then) strong, sprawling hand, divided his property, possessions and securities equally between Free and Ty and him.

Another item in the box took his eye. A long envelope with the words "To Be Opened in the Event of My Death" written across it. Curious, Thorp tore it open.

What in blinking hell . . .

The envelope contained just two papers. But just a hasty scanning of them was enough to bring Thorp Banner's world—as far as he was concerned—crashing down in ruin.

"Holy Jesus!" he exploded.

"What is it?"

Thorp didn't reply. He half-crumpled both documents in his fist before thinking better of it. Not quite believing this, he stood up and spread the papers open on the desk top, smoothing them out with unsteady hands.

"Listen to this," he said in a shaking, savage voice. "Listen now. *'To Nathan Drew, my natural son by the Navajo Horse Woman, raised as the son of my old friend and comrade Angus Drew, I bequeath—'"*

He broke off suddenly, swinging a red-eyed glare on Free. "Did you know anything about this? Goddamn you, speak up!"

Free took a step backward from the raw fury in his brother's face. "How would *I* know? Jesus, Thorp! Simmer down, will you?"

Thorp stood for a moment, looming in the lamplight, swaying a little, feeling his face contort in the surge of his boiling rage, fighting to master it. He'd never let the deep currents of his temper, powerful as they were, get out of control.

Damned if he would now!

Above all, he needed to keep his head clear.

Bending again to the documents, he read both of them through slowly and carefully, with a fierce, unbroken concentration. Meantime, Free, biting back his own burning curiosity, kept a discreet silence.

Finally, Thorp straightened up slowly, rasping a hand over his bristly jaw. "It's like this, kid." His tone was quiet now, distant and sort of musing. "We get a joint piece of Swallowtail, you and me. The south half, that is. Our *lawful* brother, old Candy Ass the painter, is relieved of any responsibility for running the outfit. No matter where he is, though, we got to see he is provided with a third of our net profits. They got to be paid semiannually and sent to him, no matter where he is." A strained pause. "We got to do all the work, that is to say, and Ty can do what he goddamn pleases—but gets to freeload off us as long as he lives."

"Jesus! Why, that ain't no way fair."

Thorp nodded musingly. "No way," he echoed. "But it seems, as the old man declares in this here *new* will, that Tyrone, having proved himself constitutionally unfit for the business of raising cattle, must be assured a due portion of his inheritance in this here manner. If old Candy Ass invests it in a proper way, it should support him in high old style for as long as need be while he makes his reputation with his art. You ever hear the beat?"

"Suppose we don't pay him a damn cent?"

"Well, sir. If you and me renege on any provisions of this will, it says here all legal-like, the executor of the old man's estate, that is Lawyer Haberstrom, is to sell off our whole goddamn share of the outfit, lock, stock and barrel, at county auction and turn the proceeds over to our *legal* brother, Nathan."

"Legal brother—" Free scowled. "Nate Drew ain't no legal brother of ours. Ain't that what that 'natural son' business means?"

"Don't matter he's legal or not." Thorp tapped the will with his forefinger. "Ain't nothing to prevent the old man leaving him whatever this paper so says. And what he's left that half-breed whelp of his is damn near half of Swallowtail. The north half."

Free's jaw dropped. "Why he can't—!"

"He's gone and done it, kid. And this will postdates the old one by three years. It's dated less than six months ago. This is the old man's own script, all right. All shaky like it's got of late."

"But Christ, Thorp! You reckon it's *true?* About that breed being—?"

"Yeah." The muscles of Thorp's face twitched. "I reckon it's true, all right. This other paper here is a deposition. It says back in the summer of 1862, Pa paid a visit to the Many Hogans Clan. He took a powerful fancy to this Injun gal. Sister

150

of Jack Lynch's squaw, she was. Wasn't till a year later Pa learned this Horse Woman had a papoose by him. That was Nate Drew. Just before he was born, Angus Drew wed the woman in the Navajo way and took her into his hogan as his second wife."

Thorp picked up the deposition and crackled it gently in his hand. "Yeah. All legal and everything. Drawn up by F. F. Haberstrom. Signed by the old man. And attested to, and witnessed, by Jack Lynch." A savage grin crooked his lips. "I make it true, sure enough. You know . . . Nate looks a smart more like Pa than you or me or Ty do. It's the Injun part that throws you off. It's so strong you never notice the rest. Yep. And I 'member that summer of sixty-two right enough. I was coming five then. Got a hazy recollection of Pa taking off for a spell to visit his old trapping haunts . . . and see his old siwash cronies. It all ties together."

"I be damned," Free whispered. "And I lay odds Ma never knew about it."

"I lay odds Nate Drew don't know about it neither. And that," Thorp said softly, "could make things a sight easier."

"How you mean?"

Thorp paced a slow circle of the floor at his slouching, big-cat walk, head bent and hands rammed in his hip pockets. Free watched him uneasily.

Still pacing, not looking up, Thorp said, "What I mean, I don't aim to share this here legacy of ours with any goddamn breed."

"Jesus, Thorp. You can't mean . . . !"

"Hear me, now." Thorp halted by the desk. "We are getting the best half of the outfit. We get the headquarters, the best range and water and all. But it don't change that a grand jag of good range is going to that breed. And that's the piece with Lynchtown on it. You think I'm gonna stand for that bunch of trash squatting on our boundary and running off our cows? Is that what *you* want?"

Free gnawed his lip worriedly. "Well . . ."

"Hell, the main reason the old man tolerated 'em is because him and Jack Lynch was friends. Nate Drew's another reason, I reckon. Pa could never come out and claim him as his own. So he must of picked this way to balm his conscience *and* protect his Injun friends, knowing I'd damn well run 'em off once Pa passed along."

Thorp paused, feeling a swollen vein ripple in his temple. His rage was carefully inheld now, but its force had turned his thoughts twisted and ugly, and he knew from Free's still-wary expression that it showed on his face.

"Look at the whole picture, kid. Pa acquired all this land, built it to the biggest outfit in the territory, back in the days of free range. He had the men who worked for him take preemption rights on big chunks of it, and he knitted it all together. You think that could be done all over in these days? Shit! We are not fixed to expand no ways, anymore. Land on all sides of us is patented to other outfits. And now the old man has cut Swallowtail clean in half. Went and saddled us with that breed and his goddamn kin as neighbors, to boot."

"Well," Free said carefully, "he is sort of kin to us too, turns out."

"Ain't he just. But maybe that will be more his bad luck than ours."

"Thorp, maybe we'd do best to just contest the will in court and—"

"That won't do," Thorp cut in irritably. "The thing is written up watertight. And you can lay odds old Haberstrom has copies of both them papers, duly signed and all, filed away . . . likely in a big city vault. It's standard practice. Won't do a lick of good, either, to try bribing Haberstrom. He's straight as an arrow, and he was Pa's good friend."

Thorp lowered his voice and leaned forward, resting his scarred knuckles on the desk. In lamplight his eyes flamed like nailheads heated to a red glow.

"I don't wait on no reading of the will, kid. I know what I want and I am set to get it. Now, you with me or not? Be no backing out later. Understand?"

Free swallowed and nodded.

CHAPTER 11

The day of Ike Banner's funeral was gray and windy. A chill north wind bit at the faces of the Swallowtail crew as they followed the wagon by twos or singly along the faint tracery of road that led to the little cemetery. Wind soughed in fitful gusts across the long-grassed slopes that were part of Ike's great ranch.

Nathan Drew rode just behind the wagon, his eyes on the rough pine box that Jim Obie, the ranch blacksmith and man-of-all-trades, had sawed and hammered together in a few hours. It was a fitting casket for the remains of the rough-hewn frontiersman Ike Banner had been.

Ike would have liked that idea. He'd have liked to see his own funeral obsequies, taking place on the land he'd owned and loved. He would have taken a wry pleasure in the spectacle.

Nathan's straight mouth relaxed at the corners. It was almost a smile. *I knew him so damned well,* he thought. *Never realized how well till now.*

It was hard to sort out his own feelings just yet. Ike's health hadn't been good these last years; the inevitable couldn't have been far off in any case. Nathan had known it. But even that knowledge hadn't prepared him for the stunning impact of Ike's death.

It had come so damned suddenly. And Ike's last words to him had been cantankerous ones. Yet Nathan didn't find that altogether unfitting. "Cantankerous" had been the word for Ike Banner nearly all his life, and the mellowing of his last years had brought Nathan a friendship closer than any he'd known.

Yes. That was the thing to remember most.

The mood of the procession was somber, and nothing in it was feigned. The men of Swallowtail had known their boss as one of them: tough but fair; a good man to work for. And they couldn't be faulted for wondering how things would work out at Swallowtail, now that Thorp was in charge.

Of course, the will was yet to be read, the property allocated to its heirs, and nobody could be sure exactly how any one of the sons would fare. But Ike was certain to have provided generously for all three. And there seemed little doubt that Thorp Banner would be the dominant voice in Swallowtail affairs, no matter how everything was divvied up.

The crew got along with Thorp, who as foreman had never shied at soiling his hands at the dirtiest and meanest of jobs, side by side with any of them. The men respected him for that. But none of them felt for him the kind of loyalty bordering on affection that they'd known for Ike.

Nothing about Thorp invited that sort of loyalty.

He was an off-ox whose nature nobody could penetrate to its core. Thorp could be tough and amiably roistering at the same time, and still make a body nervous as hell just by being around.

The three sons rode ahead of the wagon, side by side.

It was the only time Nathan could remember seeing the differences between Thorp and Ty and Free ironed out even on a surface level. All three wore sober black broadcloth, and Ty was dead sober; he'd taken a rare holiday from liquor.

The file of Swallowtail people rode up the last long slope and came to a halt outside the area of scattered wooden markers. Ike's grave, squared off next to Aunt Luella's, had been dug early this morning by a party of crewmen sent ahead. Serena and the housekeeper, Celestina, both dressed in mourning black, had brought up the rear of the procession in a buckboard. As it rolled to a stop, two crewmen handed them down from the high seat. Celestina was quietly weeping; Serena looked composed but almost deathly pale.

It had taken several hours for the cortege to reach the cemetery, but the ceremony of laying Ike Banner to his final rest was done quickly and simply. The rude coffin was lowered into the earth by four men, two on either side of the grave, holding two suspending ropes. Thorp himself read the service from the Episcopal Book of Common Prayer, and brought it off with a kind of homey dignity that Nathan noted with a twitch of irony. Thorp's big, crooked, oft-broken hands held the small volume awkwardly but gently as he read.

Thorp did a real fine job of it. Be interesting as hell, Nathan reflected, to know the run of his real thoughts as he spoke.

Maybe it was time to find out. Given Thorp's avowed feelings about him, Nathan judged with a kind of bleak fatalism that his own days at Swallowtail were numbered. Tearing up his long-time roots on the place would be difficult as hell. Might be best to bluntly confront Thorp and get it over without delay. . . .

As the file of riders headed back toward Swallowtail headquarters, leaving the party of gravediggers to fill in the grave and set the headmarker, Thorp fell into the lead. Hard to say whether he did it automatically or deliberately.

Either way, it seemed fitting.

This was as good a time as any to have it all out with him, Nathan decided. He gigged his mount forward, ranging up alongside Thorp, who gave him a somber but pleasant nod.

"Howdy, Nate. Something on your mind?"

"Sort of." Nathan felt awkward about choosing his words. "Look . . . I reckon you won't be wanting me to stay on. If that's so, I'd like to hear it said."

"You mean, seeing we have had our differences, you figure I will fire you now?"

"That's it."

Thorp brayed out his hearty laugh. "Why shit no, boy!" He reached out and clapped Nathan on the shoulder. "You think you can get shed of Swallowtail that easy, you are way off the mark. Hell, I'll even sweeten your poke with some extra pay, you consent to stay on."

Nathan narrowed his eyes to hide the astonishment he felt. "You want to keep me on?"

"Look, you just go on doing your job as good as you been doing it. Christ, man. Everyone knows you're the best damn horsebreaker in the territory. And our sideline of choosing and training horses for the army has fetched in a goodly sum over the years. You think I am about to just throw that up? All right, hell, you and I never had a love-fest going. Ain't likely we ever will. But business is business. I ain't like to ever find a better man in your trade than you are. So what about it? You staying on?"

"If you figure we can get along," Nathan said slowly.

Thorp made his laugh quiet and easy now. "We will, Nate. Don't fret none on that. You just hold up your end like you been doing, you'll get no hoorawing from me."

They rode in silence for a while.

Nathan thought it all sounded reasonable

enough, the way Thorp had put it. But he felt a wary and bewildered thread of caution, too. Maybe he, Nathan Drew, was the Indian. But it was Thorp Banner who could hate like one—as the old saying went. Still, if Thorp didn't interfere with the past routine of things, perhaps they could manage an accommodation of sorts.

One thing still bothered Nathan. Something he wouldn't let go of till he'd satisfied the matter to his own mind.

He said abruptly, "If it's all right with you, I would like to leave the party here."

Thorp raised a brow. "Mind saying why?"

"Been thinking about how your pa must have died. You said Larraldes figured a rattler might of spooked his bronc. Well, I gentled and tamed that Blackie myself. He wasn't snake shy, and he never spooked from anything. That's why I picked him for Ike's personal mount."

"Mm." Thorp rubbed his chin. "You saying he wouldn't of just run away with Pa?"

Nathan shrugged. "All I'm saying, there's an outside chance there's more to it than meets the eye. What I'd like to do is ride over to that point on the Pelado where Larraldes says he found Ike and have a look at the ground. Might be track, some sort of sign, that would show what really happened. If there is, maybe I can read it."

"Yeah. Likely you could at that," Thorp said agreeably. "All right, Nate. Best you get to it

159

before a rain or something wipes out the sign. Take all the time you need. Report to me directly you get back."

Nathan nodded and wheeled his horse away from the column.

Riding steadily on an almost due-west course, he reached the open grassy stretch just across the Swallowtail line about noon. Called the North Meadow, it was easily located because of its rough oblong shape. At one end of it the Pelado River crooked downward to angle across the northwest corner of Swallowtail range.

It was at this shallow, roiling, boulder-strewn part of the river that Larraldes had claimed he'd found Ike's body, face down in the water.

Nathan spent nearly an hour going carefully over the riverbank and the meadow itself. Afterward he wasn't quite sure what conclusions to draw. But some aspects of what he found didn't square with the gist of what Larraldes presumed had happened.

For one thing there were the horse tracks on the meadow. The sharp-dug hoofprints indicated that not one, but three hard-running horses had crossed it. The two outside horses had flanked the middle one, as if they'd raced along beside it, and suddenly they had pulled up. The middle horse—which Nathan identified as Ike's Blackie because of the bent calk on the right front shoe—had continued running. And on the side of a boulder not much farther on, Nathan found a smear of blood. Something like a falling body had crushed the grasses close to the big rock.

Nathan paid a particular attention to the riverbank where Larraldes claimed he'd found Ike lying face down in the water. A panicked Blackie might have bolted into the river and his rider might have fallen in the water after slashing the harness straps. Ike might have been knocked unconscious in the fall and then, lying face down in the water, have drowned before he revived.

It could have happened that way. Or Ike might have been knocked out before then, and his body lugged over to the river and turned face down so it would appear he'd perished in that manner. There were no horse tracks on the riverbank itself.

Still Nathan couldn't be sure. But a lot of speculative suspicion began to crowd his mind. Some of it was directed against Thorp Banner. Yet Thorp, knowing Nathan was the best tracker of his crew, had raised no objection to his inspecting the ground; he'd even been mildly encouraging.

Since he couldn't be certain of anything, Nathan decided to return to headquarters and lay out for Thorp both his findings and his doubts. Suspicions, after all, were easy to come by; shaping them into concrete terms was a sight harder. Just now Nathan found his thoughts spanning a whole range of possibilities.

He crossed the meadow and swung back toward the Swallowtail line. He hadn't gone more than a hundred yards when he saw a horseman emerging from the trees to his left. Nathan hauled up and waited.

It was Pinky Miller, the man assigned to the north line camp duty with Sixto Larraldes. Sixto had stayed over at Swallowtail for Ike's funeral today, but Miller was riding his usual rounds, it appeared. Nathan noticed, with a mild curiosity, that although Miller approached at an ambling pace, the hide of his chestnut horse was sweated as if he'd just completed a hard run.

"Howdy there, Drew." Miller showed the edge of a grin. He was a gangling man, pale and flaxen-haired, with a pinkish tinge to his eyes: a near-albino, Nathan supposed. "What brings you up this way?"

Nathan explained briefly.

"That sure is something. Could turn out to be, anyways." Miller nudged back his hat to scratch his lank colorless hair, sidling his horse a little nearer. "Where you say you saw them hard-running tracks?"

Nathan half-turned in his saddle to point, and in that instant Miller moved. His side-gun blurred out of its holster. Nathan caught the movement from the tail of his eye and came turning back, fast.

But it was too late to jerk away from the blow

or even to duck his head so its force would be partly deflected. The barrel of Miller's gun slammed full force against his temple.

Nathan felt himself tip sideways. He knew that much: He was falling. But never felt himself hit the ground.

When he came to, he knew almost at once where he was.

Back when Nathan and Ty Banner were kids, they used to explore back in the hills north of Swallowtail, and once they had come on a deserted trapper's cabin. A rundown and delapidated place even then, it had become a regular headquarters for their hiking, hunting and fishing forays back in these wild hills. He and Ty had repaired the broken door and windows and had camped overnight here quite a few times.

Groggy and sick as he was, brain reeling with a pounding headache that made him groan as he turned his head sideways, Nathan still had a quick recognition of the old place.

He was in the front room of the cabin, spreadeagled on his back. His hands and feet were anchored by rawhide thongs to the head- and footposts of a stout wooden bunk. The rest of the room was occupied by a big fieldstone fireplace, a puncheon table and a couple benches flanking it, and puncheon shelves for storing things mounted on the log walls. The walls were pierced by two windows with heavy wooden shutters that could be closed over them from inside. One opened on the south-facing wall near the door; the other was on the east wall just above the bunk where Nathan was tied.

A length of burlap sacking hung over a doorway that led to a small windowless room at the back. It, Nathan knew, contained more shelves for storage and some bunkbeds built into the walls. No sign of any life around, except for fat bluebottle flies that buzzed sluggishly around him and lighted now and then on Nathan's face, making him shake his head to dislodge them. Even that slight movement sent qualms of blinding pain through his head. He retched a couple times, rolling his head as far sideways as he could to avoid choking on his own vomit.

It was a godawful position to be fastened in.

The tightness of the thongs on his wrists and ankles—his boots had been removed—almost shut off his circulation. The thin dirty mattress under his back was stuffed with straw that poked scratchy prickles through his shirt.

Nathan judged from the slant of sunlight falling through the front window that it was late afternoon. Not much else he could tell, except that the old cabin had some tenants. The shelves were stocked with canned goods and dried staples of various kinds, and some personal gear was dumped carelessly in the corners. Quite a lot of it.

His captors must number more than one. And they were untidy in their habits.

Nathan tested his bonds and quickly concluded that fighting them would only tighten the knots and further reduce his circulation, as well as savagely lacerate his wrists. So he desisted.

Shutting his eyes against dizzying waves of pain and nausea, he tried to figure out just what had happened. Miller had cold-cocked him, and he'd been fetched to this cabin, roughly two miles from where he'd been struck down.

What else?

Pinky Miller and Sixto Larraldes were trail partners. They'd been riding a grubline when Thorp had hired the both of them—a disagreeable, often quarrelsome pair who wore their Colt pistols like badges and whom no foreman in his right mind would ordinarily take into his crew.

Miller and Larraldes were Thorp's men, hired for his own purposes. All right. Nathan had done some casual thinking on that matter long ago. Now he had cause to do some damned hard thinking on it.

Trouble was, his head was throbbing too fiercely to let him more than vaguely grope for answers. Even that raveled thread of concentration slipped away and he fell into a fitful doze. . . .

He was roused by a sound of horses coming into the yard. There was a creak of leather and rattle of bit chains; men's voices drifted through the open door. They belonged to Snake Purley and his sons, who from their talk had been out hunting. One by one they filed into the cabin.

And behind them came Thorp Banner.

"Like you told us, Mr. Banner," said Snake. "Here he is a-waiting, trussed up like a roasting bird."

Thorp crossed to one of the puncheon benches, dragged it away from the table over to the bunk and slacked onto it, elbows on knees and his big hands laced loosely together. He chewed ruminatively on a straw and grinned around it.

"Well. You got a little surprise coming to you, didn't you?"

"I had it coming," Nathan said thinly. "I turned my back on that fair-haired boy of yours."

Thorp gave a tranquil nod. "Yep. Pinky done fine. Soon as I could get away after we got back to headquarters, I rode to our north line shack and got hold of Pinky. Two of us followed you up fast as we could. Pinky surely done fine. I brought you here and went and found Snake and his boys, who was away hunting. Clear enough?"

Nathan wanted to shift against the torturing tug of the thongs on his wrists and ankles. But he was damned if he'd give Thorp that satisfaction. "Not by a far sight."

"Well, sir." Thorp took the straw from his mouth and gazed at it. "I will lay all my cards out. We opened the old man's safe last night,

Free and me did. You would never guess what we found . . ."

Nor would Nathan have guessed. But in the next few minutes he learned more than enough. He lay staring up at the smoke-blackened rafters, listening to the slugging beat of blood in his head. He felt a relentless certainty, without knowing why, that what Thorp had told him was the cold truth. Thorp allowed him a long pause to think on it.

"All right," Nathan said at last. "Why this, now? What is it you want?"

"Well, I tell you, brother." Thorp grinned and poked him in the cheek with the straw. "Say, don't that tickle your Injun risibles, now? You and me coming out to be kin! It is very simple, boy. What I, we, Free and me I mean, want is the whole outfit. Swallowtail. Lock, stock and barrel. No divvying up with a breed."

"You didn't need to knock me out and tie me up for that," Nathan said quietly. "There was a sight easier way."

Thorp eyed him blankly for a moment and then, understanding, roared and slapped his knee. "Have you bushwhacked, you mean? Then take over your chunk o' Swallowtail as next of kin? Why shoot, man! I don't have no designs on your life. All I want is for you to sign a quitclaim deed making over that north range to me. You sign it and Snake and Claud here will witness it. Then I will set you free to go any place you please to go. Long's it's a goodly way from Swallowtail. And you will go with a grand piece of money in your poke, too. Five thousand in cash."

Thorp leaned forward with a pleasant wink, giving Nathan's cheek another poke with the straw. "How's 'at sound to you, now?"

"I reckon you know the answer. Or you'd have put the offer to me flat out. Not this way."

"Well, I did allow you might prove a mite mulish. Seeing them Lynchtown friends o' yours are roosting on that north piece. Likewise, if you was minded to hold onto that range for yourself, you would be disinclined to sell. What you got to see, Nate," Thorp went on gently, "is I don't aim to see Swallowtail get split down the middle. I mean to hold it all together."

"For yourself."

"You can bet your ass on it, boy. Only real question is, how you going to make me get it? You can ride away from here in handsome shape with a fancy wad o' money in your pocket. Or . . ." Thorp paused, as if weighing his next words. "There's plenty out-of-the-way arroyos and the like back in these hills that a man's body could get dumped in and covered with rocks. Easy as pie. And he wouldn't be turned up till Judgment Day."

"I don't reckon that's a prospect that frets you a whole lot."

"What don't?"

"Judgment Day."

"Oh." Thorp threw back his head and brayed. "I declare, you do tend to talk in circles, Nate. But you talk-um with straight tongue now, huh, red brother? You got a choice. Easy way or no way at all. How's it to be?"

"What about the people in Lynchtown?"

"They got to go," Thorp replied promptly. "But I'll make it easy on 'em. They can pack out of there nice and peaceful. No reason for any fuss or muss 'less they make it."

Nathan turned his gaze back to the rafters. "I need to think on it."

Thorp chuckled. "On how stubborn a bastard you aim to be? Sure, go ahead."

"Speaking of bastards."

"What?"

"Difference between you and me is, I couldn't help being one."

Thorp brayed some more. "Say, that's good. That's real fine-haired, boy. All right, you think on it a day or so. Till I get that quitclaim deed drawn up. I will go to a lawyer real soon and be back here the day after." Thorp paused meaningfully. "I have always took you for a real bone-deep hardhead, Nate. I surely hope I been wrong all this time."

Thorp rose from the bench and tramped outside, followed by Snake and his sons. They stood in the yard and conversed in normal tones, the words carrying plainly to Nathan.

"Give him food and water," said Thorp. "Unloose him when he has got to relieve himself, but all of you keep guns on him meantime. Afterward you tie him up again like he is."

"It is what you say, Mr. Banner," said Snake. "You reckon he will be minded to go along like you want?"

"Well," Thorp said in a speculative tone, "you just never know about some critters, Snake. Man can get set up in the damnedest ways in his own head, even given he is a breed. See, if a man's got a quarter of Injun blood in his veins, that makes him legally an Injun. The gov'ment says so. Nate, now—he is half Injun. Being legally a redskin don't give ole Nate much of a leg to stand on, come to property rights. He ain't no citizen of the United States—just a ward of the gov'ment. And leave me tell you, Nate Drew is no simpleton. He will see there is a strong chance that no federal or state court in this territory would recognize any property claim of his. He will allow that in his thinking."

"That do sound like fine sense, Mr. Banner. And iffen he signs this here deed, you will jest turn him loose?"

"Why not?" If a man could inject a casual shrug into the tone of his voice, Thorp did it right then. "I want everything done nice and legal.

170

After all, Snake, he is blood kin to us Banners, come to find out. I don't need to tell a ole boy from the Ozarks like you how a man feels about kin. Damn, no. I don't aim to hurt this breed no ways 'less he makes me."

"Mr. Banner, that talk rings purely fine. Us, we don't hold him no grudge neither. Though he done us a little bit of dirt a spell back."

"You better not," Thorp said gently. "I don't want to find no marks on him that shouldn't be there when I come back here in maybe a couple days."

"No, sir. Don't you worry 'bout that. Just a couple things I wonder. Won't he be missed if he don't show up back at your outfit shortly?"

Thorp laughed. "Why no. Hell no, Snake. Nate Drew is always been a lonesome sort o' cuss. Even lives in a shack by himself on our place. Sometimes he would go off two-three days at a time by himself, hunting maybe, or visiting his siwash relatives over in Lynchtown. Pa, he always tolerated just about anything Nate done. Now we know why."

"Ain't it the truth. Other thing I wondered, supposing you turn him loose and later on he chooses to come back and tell folks what really happent?"

Thorp's rich chuckle again. "He could do that, sure. But who'd believe him? Who'd even give a hoot? Breed's word don't count for a damn in the courts o' this territory. Like I told you, Snake. One thing he ain't is dumb . . ."

Nathan listened to the sounds of Thorp mounting his horse and riding out of the yard.

The conversation had been staged for his benefit, he knew. No doubt Thorp and Snake had talked it out beforehand. It was a neat mixture of facts and possible truths, designed for Nathan's overhearing.

Did Thorp have any real intention of freeing him once he signed the petition? Nathan answered his own question: *Why should he?*

What Thorp had told Snake Purley about the legal status of Indians in this territory was in no way exaggerated. Even so, as long as Thorp's unwanted half-breed brother remained alive, he might, in some way that Thorp couldn't yet anticipate, prove to be a nuisance.

Thorp might put on a crude front, but his mind was always shrewd and searching, accustomed to ferreting out every potential facet of any situation. Nathan did not believe for a moment that his avowed sense of kinship with a "breed" was heartfelt. Dead and buried in some unknown arroyo, Nathan Drew would simply drop out of sight—and nobody the wiser. Thorp's story that Nathan had sold out his piece of Swallowtail and then departed the country might be doubted by some . . . but who could prove anything?

Nevertheless, if Nathan were to mysteriously

drop out of sight suddenly after Ike Banner's death, a lot of suspicion could come to bear on Thorp. It might lead to embarrassing complications. To Thorp, getting Nathan's signature on that quitclaim deed could mean a fairly sure way of circumventing a possible investigation. Even if Nathan were "only a breed," it would be sensible for Thorp to be able to offer a solid explanation for Nathan's sudden exodus of the country. If any questions were asked, Thorp would only need to bring out the deed with Nathan's signature.

As these thoughts revolved through Nathan's pounding head, the Purleys came back into the cabin.

Ignoring him, they began preparations for supper, laying kindling wood in the fireplace and getting out a blackened iron stew-pot, along with some dried fruits and fresh wild greens. Claud gutted and beheaded and skinned a fresh-killed rabbit.

None of them had much to say, but now and then as they worked—taking an occasional pull at a jug of what Nathan supposed was homemade hooch—the Purleys would turn brief glances on their captive. Each of them had the same stony, bleach-eyed look that told him nothing at all.

Once Sheb said venomously, "I could kill that son-of-a-bitching breed. I could send him to glory easy as falling off a log."

"You sure could, son," Snake said amiably. "You could get the shit kicked out of you just that easy, too."

Lying on the prickly straw tick, with flies buzzing all around and sometimes settling on him, his limbs stretched taut and sweat soaking his clothes, Nathan felt an increasing misery. His thirst was becoming unbearable.

Finally he said in a scratchy voice, "I believe you were told to give me water."

Snake was crouched by the fireplace, ready to strike a match and touch it to a heap of kindling wood. "Sakes alive," he said, scratching his chin. "I recall we was told something of that sort."

Rising off his hunkers, he walked over to a bucket by the door, thrust a tin dipper into it and brought the dipper up brimming with water. He drank it down with a noisy show of appreciation. Then he filled the dipper again and walked over to the bunk. Slowly and deliberately, Snake poured all the water out on the packed-clay floor.

Grinning, he watched Nathan's face.

"There you go, breed. A whole dipper of water and more where that come from. All the water you want, iffen you can get down there and lap 'er up."

CHAPTER 12

Ty Banner did no drinking on the day of his father's funeral. The craving flickered on and off at the back of his mind, but it was curiously dulled, as if the connection between appetite and nervous system had been severed. In fact, he did feel numb and apathetic. He made a pretense at eating supper, but had no hunger for food either.

Afterward Ty went to his and Serena's room, lighted the lamp on the commode and stared into the mirror at his puffy, ravaged face.

I guess I did care a lot for the old man, he thought. He tried to understand me . . . at the last. He tried. And what did I give him back? Thorp and Free and me. What did any of us give him?

Suddenly grief stabbed him like a knife through the numbness. The image in the mirror blurred and he felt a sob choke up in his throat. *Pa . . . Pa!*

The delayed shock of pain hit Ty full force. And it released the familiar craving like a tugged trigger. There was a half-empty bottle around here somewhere . . . he'd cached it somewhere in his last night's stupor. Savagely he yanked open a drawer of the commode and rummaged through it. Then another. Had Serena found it and hidden it, damn her?

He scrabbled through a nest of her underthings. And then stopped abruptly.

Beneath the array of dainty garments he found a thick sheaf of papers. Ty stared unbelievingly. They were drawings and sketches of his, all in various states of delapidation. He took them out and leafed through them with shaking fingers. Each one was a piece of work he had torn and crumpled up, then discarded, in one drunken or frustrated rage or another. Each had been neatly mended and pressed flat. A full dozen of them.

The door opened behind him and Serena came in. She halted on the threshold. Her reflection in the mirror stared at him. Slowly Ty turned to face her, holding out the thick sheets of artist's stock.

"You . . . *saved* these?"

Somehow he found this incomprehensible.

Serena came swiftly forward and almost snatched the sheaf of drawings from his hand. Spots of high color burned in her cheeks. "You threw them away, didn't you? Now they're mine!"

"But why—"

"Why not? What else do I have of you anymore, Ty?"

The flare of spirit in her face, her voice, left him speechless for a moment. For his gentle wife, he knew, this amounted to an intensity of anger.

"Oh, See. My God."

Ty clasped a hand over his face, leaning back against the commode. Words formed on his tongue, *I'm sorry*. But he left them unsaid. He had said them too many sorry times.

He dropped the hand from his face. It was shaking badly now. He swung back to the commode and pulled open another drawer; there was the bottle. Serena turned back to the door.

"See." He walked over to her and handed the bottle to her. "Pour that out. Get rid of it."

She studied his face quietly, almost impersonally. "Are you sure?"

"I'm sure."

"It's been a long time since you've gotten through a night without it."

"I'll get through this one without it." He forced a faint, crooked smile to his lips. "There's no more of it on the place. None that's mine, anyway. I'd have gone to town and renewed my supply today . . . if not for Pa. Go on, See. Get rid of it now."

Uncertainly, she looked at the bottle in one of her hands, the sheaf of drawings in the other, and then back at Ty.

Understanding, he nodded wearily. "Put 'em back. They'll be safe. I won't touch a one."

Silently she returned the sketches to the drawer, then walked out and softly closed the door.

Ty undressed and blew out the lamp, and lay down in the dark.

It would be a long night for sure. The craving came and went in waves, squeezing sweat from the hollows of his body. But if there's nothing to drink, I can't drink it. So I'll go without. All tonight and tomorrow. If I can make it through then, Pa, I'll have a start.

Just a start.

Meantime it was going to be a hell of a long night.

After tossing and turning for a while, the want of liquor raging like a fever through his brain and bowels, Ty got up in the dark and found the water pitcher on the commode. He picked it up and drained it. The water filled his belly and killed some of the thirst. Made it a little more bearable, anyway. Afterward he was able to lie quietly, even falling into a nervous doze. . . .

He woke suddenly out of a sounder sleep than he would have believed possible. Next him in the bed was movement and warmth. Female flesh, naked and close and yielding, as he could not remember it for a long time. God. How long since he had savored it with the tingling, undulled senses of a sober man?

"See?"

"Yes. Is it very bad, darling?"

"Not too bad. Not now."

He felt the surrendering of her flesh, the throb

and swell of his own, and the tang of full, rising desire. It would not be such a long night after all.

Ty was up and almost fully dressed when Serena awoke the next morning. She sat up in amazement, the bedclothes tumbling to her lap. "Ty? *You're* up already?"

He finished adjusting his cravat and turned from the mirror. "Surprise, huh? Gad, but you're a fetching baggage, even by daylight. Nothing like a state of utter deshabille to bring out a girl's, um, assets."

Serena blushed and pulled the bedclothes up to her shoulders. She smiled a little, but her eyes were dark with anxiety. "How do you feel?"

"Never better. But it's not the mornings I have to worry about. Not too much."

She nodded gravely. It was always later in the day that Ty's heavy drinking began. Around noon or so was when today's hell would begin. And how many days of hell would follow? Ty couldn't be sure. He'd quit the bottle for a while on other occasions. But never after such a prolonged period of heavy day-to-day drinking. This latest debauch of his had lasted nearly a year.

"Anyway—" He shrugged into his coat as he came over to the bed, bent and kissed her. "It's something just to greet the dawn feeling like a million for once. Well—say a few hundred thousand. Take me a spell to work back up the scale."

"M'm—" She leaned away from his kiss, demurely. "Are you sure you didn't get up a bit *too* early?"

Ty laughed and went back to the commode. He opened the drawer containing the sketches and thumbed briefly through them. "You said these are yours now, eh?"

"I did. And they are."

"Well, I wondered if you might waive rights on at least one. This."

He showed it to her: a remarkable study of young Sandal Cruz dressed in his *vaquero's* outfit. The lines and strokes of the sketch were energetic and vivid, bringing out the boy's vitality and ebullient youth with a wonderful clarity. Looking at it now, Ty could soberly verify his opinion that it was one of the best things he'd produced in a long time.

"Thought the kid might like to have it. Would you mind?"

"Why darling, of course not. It will be a wonderful gift for Sandal." A puckish little smile touched Serena's lips. "But what else do you have in mind today? I know you're eager to get on with *something*. I can always tell when you are."

With a kind of sheepish grin, Ty admitted that he'd been toying for some time with the notion of riding out to a place called Piegan Canyon that lay a ways west of the headquarters. There was a part of the vast gorge whose walls formed a vivid stratification that he'd long thought would make an ideal subject for a spectacular landscape in oils.

Maybe, for once, he could summon the energy to get over to that canyon and make some preliminary sketches, if nothing else. And repeated visits to the place would occupy him for days to come.

Serena didn't have to be told that it would also provide an ongoing diversion from the temptation of booze, if he could manage it. "That sounds fine," she enthused quietly. "But you shan't go off without a good breakfast. And I'll make some sandwiches to see you through the day."

She was well aware that once Ty became absorbed in his work, he might keep laboring through the whole day and think of nothing else, not even food. But if he did think of it, he'd be as hungry as the devil—and he was usually a hearty eater. Ty had to smile at the thought. Serena knew his thoughts and moods and feelings. She understood his pleasures and his pains as nobody ever had.

How easily he'd forgotten all that. For too damned long, he thought soberly. I won't let it happen again. Damn it, I won't!

Afterward, with a solid breakfast under his

belt, Ty walked down to the corrals. Both old Diego and young Sandal Cruz were over by the breaking corral, readying for the day's work. Sandal would be riding the kinks out of some proddy broncs under his grandfather's watchful eye. But there would be no more rough-breaking of the real *ladinos* until Nathan Drew returned to give the orders.

Ty gave Sandal a brusque order. "Hitch up one of the buckboards. I'm riding out today."

"*Si, patron*! Right away."

Sandal headed for the carriage shed.

"How's he doing with those rough ones?" asked Ty.

Diego shrugged. "*Poco á poco.*" He cast a shrewd, questioning look at Ty. "You up pret' early today, Señor."

Ty managed a self-conscious grin. "Could be. Um, by the way—" He laid the articles he was carrying on the ground, then unrolled the sketchpaper with its full-length study of Sandal. "Here's something you might give the kid. Knocked it out the other day. Then threw it away—see where it got torn?—but afterward I got thinking Sandal might like to have it."

Old Diego gave the sketch a long careful scrutiny, the leathery wrinkles deepening at the corners of his eyes. "Ah, h'm. Yes, this I think he will like ver' much. But maybe, *patrón*, you should give it to him yourself. Eh?"

"Maybe I should at that." As he carefully rolled up the sketch again, Ty couldn't resist adding, "Like I told Nate Drew. I did figure that grandson of yours has some natural ability as an art critic."

Thorp was over by the blacksmith shop helping Jim Obie, the smith, reshoe Thorp's favorite mount when Ty came rattling by in the buckboard. He looked chipper as hell this morning, thought Thorp. Even seemed in a reasonably decent mood. Damned strange, that.

Thorp raised a hand for him to pull up. As Ty reined in the team, Thorp walked over to the wagon and leaned his crossed arms on the wagon box, saying genially, "Well, if you ain't bright-eyed as a badger today. What's up? Going to town to lay in more booze?"

"Nothing that hilarious," said Ty. "I'm going to do a bit of sketching. Over at Piegan Canyon."

"For sure?" Thorp glanced down at the wagon bed. "Oh. Got your day's ration of firewater in that flour sack, huh?"

"If you want to think so."

With a word to the horses, Ty put them in motion again. Thorp scratched his chin and gazed thoughtfully after his brother. Then he turned to the smith. "Finish up the shoeing, Jim. I got other chores to see to."

Thorp headed for the bunkhouse.

This was the chance he had waited on, and there was no hesitation in him. Not that he'd decided right off the bat that Tyrone had to be put out of the way ("out of his misery" was how Thorp phrased it to himself), but once the conviction took root in his mind, it was fixed as irrevocably as death.

Ty's death.

Alive, Ty would be a blood-sucking leech on the life of Swallowtail for years to come. That knowledge, and the stipulation in the old man's will that covered it, had left as venomous a fury burning in Thorp as the revelation that Nathan Drew would fall heir to a vast chunk of the outfit. Fed by a few hours of hot brooding, his rage had erupted into decision.

Ty was drinking himself to death anyway. His life was worth about as much as teats on a boar. But how long might it last? A heavy-drinking man only in his mid-twenties could have a lot more years remaining to him. He might even straighten up and abandon the bottle.

And Thorp wasn't disposed to wait on what *might* happen. He'd waited too damned many years already. He wanted it all. All of Swallowtail, and he wanted it now, as he'd told Free.

What he hadn't told Free were his plans for Ty.

Free was a weak-kneed ninny, sure enough. No damned strength of character at all. He'd never consent to the murder of Ty with the same malleable ease as he had to getting rid of Nate Drew. So Ty's death had to look like a complete accident. Even Free must be satisfied it was an accident. The only question was—how?

Now Ty himself had presented the answer. *Piegan Canyon!* Ty had set it up for him better than anything Thorp himself could have arranged by devious trickery. And the opportunity had come far sooner than he'd hoped.

Free would be safely out of the way most of the day. Thorp had sent him to town with a passel of the necessary papers to have a quit-claim deed drawn up. It would be quietly done through a shyster lawyer who was a poker-playing acquaintance of theirs.

The crew had been dispatched to their day's duties, and only Sixto Larraldes and Jim Obie remained at headquarters. Thorp had told Sixto not to return to the line shack right away. To lay over here for a day or so, as he might have a job for him.

Thorp opened the door of the bunkhouse, went through the cramped room where the crew's gear and belongings were stored, and into the long bunkroom. Larraldes was sprawled on a bunk, smoking, leafing idly through a tattered, dog-eared mail-order catalogue. Sixto couldn't read English, but one section of the catalogue was devoted to pictures of full-blown ladies in corsets and other underthings, and all the boys enjoyed looking at those.

"All right," Thorp told him curtly. "Listen now."

Sixto laid the catalogue aside and swung his stocky frame out of the bunk. Sleepy-eyed, *cigarillo* tucked between his thin lips, he squinted at Thorp through the smoke.

"I'm listen'," he said lazily.

From the window of the ranch office, Thorp watched Sixto ride out from the headquarters. He was following the road to town due west. But watching for the place where the wheel tracks of Ty's buckboard turned off toward Piegan Canyon, Sixto would turn off too and follow those.

Sixto had all the orders he would need. And Thorp had advised him to take his time. To watch for just the right moment. The more it looked like an accident, the better. Being damned efficient in his own way, and having somewhat less conscience than a rattlesnake, Sixto would follow instructions to the letter.

Thorp slacked into Ike's creaking swivel chair, propped his boots on the desk and folded his arms behind his head. He rocked gently back and forth, grinning. Yessir . . . it was all in motion now. Best to have it over in one quick continuous stroke. Ty. Nate Drew.

And Jack Lynch.

Nathan had to go, certainly. And Ty. The way Thorp had rigged it, with Ty meeting his end in an unmistakable accident, would remove any shadow of suspicion of his brothers' complicity. But it would seem damned ominous, once the terms of Ike's will and the accompanying deposition were made public, if Nate Drew were also suddenly to turn up dead, no matter how cleverly the "accident" was arranged.

For that reason Thorp was determined to extract a signed quitclaim deed from Nathan before putting him out of the way for good. Once the deed was in his hands, it could be given out that Nathan had signed over his inherited property to Thorp and Freeman Banner for the sum of five thousand dollars and had then departed the country. Yessir. It should all fit together like clockwork. People might have their suspicions, but what the hell could anyone prove?

That left just one thing. Jack Lynch.

Lynch had signed the deposition. Likely he also knew about the provisions of Ike's last will and testament. Jack Lynch had been Ike's closest friend and confidant. Thorp's mind skirted restlessly, uneasily around that fact, probing at it carefully. Jack Lynch knew too damned much. And maybe far more than even the will and deposition revealed.

With the ponderous certainty of a massive roof beam settling into place, Thorp made a final touchy decision. Lynchtown had to go, of course; he'd long ago made up his mind to that. But he'd thought there was no reason to hurry.

Now he thought there was. Jack Lynch had to go too. But not alive.

Obviously, the best way to take out Lynchtown was by a night attack. Why not tonight? The crew would come off range duty while it was still daylight. He would issue the orders and they would follow them. Thorp had no doubt of it. Everyone knew what a stinking pesthole Lynchtown was. That its inhabitants were squatting on patented Swallowtail range. If that weren't enough, Thorp had a real clincher in mind.

In the end, not a man would object to wiping Lynchtown off the map.

Thorp's boots thumped to the floor. He stood up. The swelling exultance he felt, the anticipation of crushing almost in one stroke every major obstacle to his ambitions, fed his growing sense of power like a draft of strong liquor.

He laughed aloud. The heat of his thoughts took a sharp twist. Lust crackled in his head like sudden flame.

Sunday, it was. The housekeeper, Celestina, would be attending Mass and spending the day with her relatives over at town, in the Mexican quarter. He was alone in the house . . . except for Serena.

Damn! Why not?

It was great sport just to frighten hell out of Ty's wife. But her piteous fear of him had only deepened Thorp's desire to hammer it forcibly home. He laughed again. He hadn't drunk a drop, but the feeling of triumph that surged through him was more savagely intoxicating than any ordinary spirits.

Serena was a creature of habit. Usually, about this time of the morning, after breakfast and some early chores were done, she would go to her room and take her time about changing from robe and gown, then grooming and dressing herself for the day.

Thorp tramped out of the office, across the back parlor and into the sleeping wing of the sprawling house. His boots clattered loudly in the hallway as he entered it; he didn't give a damn how much noise he made.

At Ty and Serena's room he paused, then grasped the doorknob and flung the door wide open.

Serena turned wildly to face him. She wore nothing but her drawers and a camisole which she was in the act of buttoning. Hanging partly open under her nerveless fingers, it showed the satiny cleft between the pale mounds of her breasts.

The naked fright in her face pleased Thorp more than the sight of her half-naked body.

"Nice," he drawled. "Can't stand having a sloppy-ass woman about. Real nice the way you get all gussied up of a morning, See honey. Only maybe the proceedings will be delayed for a spell today. What you think of that, now? Huh?"

Grinning, Thorp stepped into the room and kicked the door shut behind him.

CHAPTER 13

For Lolly Hosteen the trouble had begun when her grandfather had caught her swimming naked and otherwise carrying on with one of the young men of the village. Jack Lynch's patience had reached an end. He'd tied her to a tree and used a harness strap on her back and buttocks.

She could live in a white world or in an Indian world, he'd often told her. It would have to be one or the other. She must make her choice and then abide by the rules of whichever way of life she chose. But the sort of raw, unaccountable behavior into which she'd fallen must come to an end. Or she herself would come to an end and it would be a bad one.

Now Jack Lynch had driven the lesson home with a vengeance.

Sobbing with rage, yelling defiant imprecations, Lolly had packed up her few belongings and a supply of food and tied them on one of her two ponies. Then she mounted the other pony and rode away from Lynchtown, leading the pack-horse with her worldly possessions.

She hadn't gone far before a measure of sanity had cooled her perspective. Exactly where could she go? She knew nobody outside of Lynchtown, other than Nathan Drew and Ike Banner—and she wasn't about to throw herself on the mercy of either. The world outside of Lynchtown, other than the wilderness around it, was a mystery to her. Her fleeting thought of going to a white man's town and trying to make her own way quickly curdled.

The realization that eventually she must return to Lynchtown settled in her with a leaden bitterness. All *right,* damn it! She would have to go back. But not right away. She had plenty of grub and she had a rifle to fetch game. She knew the country around Lynchtown, the woods and meadows, the flats and foothills, and she could live off it for a long time.

Let them worry about her back in Lynchtown, meantime. By God, they'd be sorry. At least a few people would be. Mostly she wanted Jack Lynch to suffer a little. After the first flare of hate subsided, she grudgingly conceded that she did love the old man. Could even see his side of the matter. But he had hurt her and coming from someone you cared for, a whipping hurt twice as much.

Twenty-four hours later, the weals across her back and rear still made Lolly shudder with their fiery ache. Jack Lynch had not broken skin. But he still had a strong arm, and he'd laid on the strokes with a will. When she stripped down to bathe in a spring-fed pool that morning, she could see, peering over her shoulder, that the livid stripes on her tender tawny flesh would be a long time healing.

Lolly had made her camp at the crown of a wooded hill, in a small clearing. When she built a fire to cook her grub, she was careful to keep it small and almost smokeless. Her mood remained smoldering and sullen, and she did not want to be found by anybody. One side of the hill terminated in a gaunt granite spur from which she had a panoramic view of the country for a long way around, and she had a pair of field glasses to help her study it.

Once she saw the three Purleys hunting along a creek not far to the west. Lolly knew who they were and what they were, and she suspected they were the ones who'd been high-grading Swallowtail beef. It would have been easy for the Lynchtowners to intercept whoever was doing it, but any Indian or breed would be a fool to bear witness against a white man. For that reason Jack Lynch had sent only a cautious report on the matter to Ike Banner; what Ike chose to do about it was his business. Evidently he'd done nothing as yet.

Lolly caught sight of the Purleys a few more times, singly or together, over the next couple days. She made certain of their whereabouts because she planned to do a little hunting herself, and wanted to be sure her gunfire wouldn't bring them down on her. Lolly was like a shadow in the woods. It was easy to slip anywhere around and past these white peckerwoods whenever she felt like it. Also, it was fun to spy on them from not far off. The streak of truant recklessness in her nature made her discount any risk.

Late on the second day Lolly saw Thorp Banner pay a visit to the Purleys' cabin, and that aroused her interest. She knew the Purleys had been fired from Swallowtail and that the old trapper's cabin lay beyond that outfit's north boundary. So why was Thorp paying a call on them? It looked like a friendly visit, all of them chatting amiably enough outside the cabin.

From her position in the pines on a nearby ridge, Lolly could focus their faces clearly in the powerful glasses. She even tried to read their lips, but with no success.

Anyway Thorp didn't stay long. He mounted up and rode away, and the Purleys went back into the cabin. Soon smoke of their supper fire curled up from the stone chimney.

Lolly was idly curious and she had little to do with her time except indulge that curiosity. Maybe tomorrow . . .

It was the second day of his captivity. In one day and night Nathan Drew had learned what honest-to-God misery was.

The door and hinged windows of the cabin were propped open at this midday hour to admit any vagrant breeze. There wasn't any, however. The baking heat rose in shimmering waves off the trampled floor of the clearing outside; the leaves of aspen Nathan could see through the door and window openings hung drooping and motionless.

He was broiling in his own sweat. The flies no longer buzzed erratically around his prone form; they settled and crawled on his flesh, his sweat-drenched clothing. His head still throbbed sickly from Miller's blow, and the flesh was raw and sticky where his scalp had been laid open. The flies worried the wound incessantly, maddeningly. All he could do to discourage them was violently shake his head. And it hurt like hell.

Because Thorp had ordered them to do so, the Purleys periodically loosened his bonds so he could go outside and relieve himself. Also at long intervals they gave him a little water and permitted him a few mouthfuls of food. Afterward they would cinch him up as tightly as before, in the same position.

Nathan had read about how medieval torturers used to stretch their victims on the rack. His own situation just now couldn't be too far from that of those sorry souls. His bones were intact, but the rawhide thongs were cruelly tight and were drawn so fast to the four posts that the blood flow in his hands and feet was all but cut off for hours at a time. The flesh of his extremities was swollen and discolored, almost unfeeling. He knew from the brief trips outside that his wrists and ankles were bloodily raw, like the scalp wound.

Thorp was supposed to return today or tomorrow. A little more of this and his right hand would be in no condition to sign that quitclaim deed, even was he minded to.

Nathan had no idea what he would do. He might insist, as a condition of signing, that he be set definitely free and equipped with a horse and gun before he consented to put his signature to the document. Yes, he might do that. But the chance that Thorp would accede to such a demand was thin. Damned thin indeed . . .

Nathan twisted in his sweating agony. He was tortured by an overpowering thirst, but it would be useless, just now, to try rousing the Purleys. All three of them were soddenly snoring in the back room, dead drunk and passed out.

They'd made a long, merry night of swilling down rotgut and meantime tormenting their prisoner with such indignities as they dared inflict on him. Thorp had warned them about not marking him up, so they were chary about going too far. But it had been hours since Nathan had relieved himself and just as long since he'd taken a sip of water. His few attempts to arouse the bastards, croaked out of his whetstoned throat, had brought no response.

The Purleys were dead to the world, and they might remain that way for many hours.

What difference would it make? A thickness of despair had locked on Nathan's brain long since. The mere budge of his thoughts was like a trickle of muddy molasses, a stir of nightmare sensations that made no sense at all. Except for one thing: Soon Thorp Banner would return. And then—

Quite suddenly, without warning, the hot fly-fretted monotony was broken. In about the last way he would have expected.

In the window just above the bunk where he lay bound, a face appeared. It was Lolly Hosteen. She was peering into the half-shadowed room, and now her eyes turned downward. She saw Nathan; her mouth opened in a shock of surprise.

At least that's what he thought he saw. Maybe it was an hallucination.

But Lolly spoke, sharp and sudden: *"Nate!"*

"Keep it down—"

Still only half-believing, he husked the warning at her. Lolly crouched lower, her eyes darting back and forth as they barely cleared the sill.

Roused to full wakefulness now, Nathan wasted no time. He didn't ask Lolly what had brought her here; he didn't care. A lift of excited hope flared in him. As quickly as he could, he explained the situation, keeping his voice at a whisper and leaving out unnecessary details. But was careful to stress that the Purleys were asleep in the next room.

"You can get inside now," he said, "and cut me loose. But make it fast, will you? And don't make any noise."

Lolly's response was to push out her lips and give him a long, brooding study. "Now," she whispered, "just why the hell should I do that?"

Nathan stared at her.

"This is no time for games, girl. Maybe you don't understand. My head's on the block."

"Oh, yeah? Am I supposed to cry about that?" Lolly's whisper was very low and fierce; it held a bite of genuine anger. "You know what I am doing out here, Nathan Drew? That damn Jack Lynch give me a hiding. He whipped hell out of me and he drove me out of Lynchtown."

"I can't believe that. Jack wouldn't . . ."

"The hell he wouldn't! He done it. Ole Grampaw ranks as heap big chief in your book, don't he? Well, I don't owe him nothing, and I don't owe you nothing! I ain't forgot how you treated me. Maybe I oughta just leave you like you are. What you think of that?"

Nathan couldn't quite believe what he was hearing. Lolly was wild and unpredictable, full of moods and whims. He'd known that from a long time back. But no matter how justified she felt in her rage against Jack Lynch, she wouldn't just . . . !

"Listen." Nathan made his whisper gentle. "I know how you must feel just now. But—"

From the back room came a heavy groan, then the *clunk* of a man's booted feet hitting the floor as he swung out of a bunk. Sheb Purley said, thick-voiced, "Hey, brother. Where you going?"

"Take a pee," Claud replied just as thickly.

"Uh . . . okay. Guess I will too."

Lolly ducked back and away from the window, dropping out of sight fast. The Purley sons came lurching out of the back room, looking rumpled and bleary-eyed. Snake went on snoring in his bunk.

"How about me?" Nathan managed to croak. "I got to go pretty bad."

The two halted and stared at him owlishly.

"Hell with you, breed," said Sheb.

Claud worked a hand through his matted hair, scowling. "We better take him out. Pappy will raise hell if he messes up that tick. Get your gun and hold it on him. Fetch mine too."

Sheb got their Colts from the sleeping room and handed Claud his, yawning prodigiously and holding his own revolver loosely trained on Nathan as Claud untied the thongs from the bunkposts, leaving them dangling from Nathan's wrists. Nathan was scarcely able to maneuver to his feet. Each time he'd been freed of his bonds he had found it harder to force his cramped and leaden limbs to movement. His legs nearly folded under him as Claud pushed him stumbling toward the door.

If Lolly meant to help him, now was her chance. But Snake was still in the cabin. If he should wake up when Lolly made her play, it could be disastrous. She would have to get all three Purleys under her gun at once. . . .

Out in the yard Nathan came to a stop. He turned to face his captors. "All right," he said calmly. "I decided."

"Huh?" said Claud.

"I am ready to talk turkey about that quitclaim. But not to you. Go bring your pa out."

Claud backed carefully away from Nathan, holding his pistol leveled. "Roust Pa out, Sheb. Tell him the breed is getting some smarts. Maybe you gonna stay alive after all, breed."

Nathan stretched his cracked lips in a piece of a smile. "Maybe."

Muttering to himself, Sheb went back in the cabin.

The sun beat heavily into the clearing, its slanting rays hot against Nathan's back and head. The warmth reached pleasantly to his blood, quickening its sluggish flow, sharpening all his senses. He swung on his heel and began to pace slowly back and forth, flexing his fingers. Idly, he let his gaze stray across the banked brush that flanked the clearing's edge.

No sign of Lolly. But there wouldn't be any until she cared to show herself. *If she does!*

"You stay still now, breed," Claud ordered

flatly. "Take your pee if you want. But don't get moving around like that."

Snake came out of the cabin, Sheb trotting behind him. Snake was holding a dipper of water in both hands, gulping thirstily from it, the drops running off his beard. He lowered it and drew a sleeve across his mouth, glaring at Nathan.

"Well? You ready to make medicine?"

"Just about," said Nathan. "There's a few things that bother me."

Snake was not armed, he saw. Also he looked as sluggish and hungover as his sons. That would help. But Nathan wanted the attention of all three men fixed on him. He began pacing up and down again, feeling their eyes follow him.

"Don't mind if I move about some, do you? Got to limber up and get my blood moving if I'm to sign anything."

Snake nodded impatiently. "Move all you want. But do it slow, damn slow. Now. Suppose you say what is taking your fancy."

"Just a few things. I will sign that deed when Mr. Banner shows up with it." Nathan steadily flexed his hands. "But I don't aim to put up with any more abuse while I am waiting. I want a good meal. The best you can whip together. All the water I can drink and a few slugs of that rotgut of yours. No more being trussed up like a beast for the slaughter. I want to clean up and I want a good long sleep. No more hoorawing by you and your boys. Meantime, you can keep all the guns on me you want."

"We can?" Snake slapped his thigh and let out an explosive cackle. "You hear *that,* boys? You hear all them fine and fancy things this breed tells us we *can* do?"

Claud and Sheb glanced at each other, at their father, at Nathan. They grinned uncertainly.

Nathan's up-down walk had shifted gradually from the middle of the clearing to the west side of it, even as he was talking. Without thinking, the Purleys slightly turned to keep facing him. Now the backs of all three men were to the east flank of the clearing . . . where Lolly had been. They were all watching him, incredulity mixing with their amusement.

Lolly made her move, stepping silent as a ghost out of the brush at their backs. Her Winchester rifle was lifted and not quite butted against her shoulder.

"Any of you turn around," she said quietly, "and he will be a dead 'un 'fore he can bat a winker."

The expressions on their faces were almost comical just then. But no matter how badly they were surprised, all three recognized the note of icy menace in the girl's voice. Half drunk as they still were, all had the presence of mind not to move. They stood flatfooted and foolish, blinking.

"You with the guns, drop 'em. Then step away from them."

"Pappy?" Sheb's voice held a panicked half-whine.

Cautiously, Snake turned his head enough for his bloodshot vision to pick up Lolly from the tail of his eye. What he saw, of course, was a tall, thin girl in her teens. But unless he were blind, he couldn't miss the easy, professional way she held that rifle pointed. And Lolly did not look soft. There was nothing soft in her stare or her stance. Only the tone of her voice was gentle, and that was iced with warning.

"You best do like you're told, boys." Snake blinked groggily. "Howdy there, missy. Ain't seen you nowheres about before."

"I been about," Lolly said matter-of-factly. "Didn't choose to be seen, so you didn't see me. Suppose you do like you are told, *boys*. Fine. Now you shucked them guns, all o' you move off from them. Move to your left. That's right."

Nathan, still unsteady on his feet, was already moving forward to pick up the pistols discarded by Claud and Sheb.

As Nathan bent over to pick up the Colts, Claud, who was the one nearest him, exploded into action. He flung himself sideways and into Nathan, carrying him to the ground.

In the ensuing confusion, as he wrestled with Claud, Nathan was dimly aware that both Snake and Sheb had wheeled around and were lunging at Lolly. Her rifle roared. Sheb went down like an axed steer.

Just as quickly, Lolly levered the Winchester and swung it toward Snake. But he reached her in the same instant and, with a swing of his arm, smacked her gunbarrel aside even as she fired. The bullet missed his hip by an inch or so. And then Snake, cursing and yelling unintelligibly, was trying to wrest the rifle from her hands.

Rolling in the dirt with Claud, both of them fighting to get hold of one of the pistols, Nathan caught only fleeting notices of Lolly's predicament. He was still stiff and weak from all the hours of being tied down, his hands numb from the bite of thongs. His only chance against the husky and sizable Claud was to get his hands on a gun before Claud did. Nathan threw every atom of concentration into that single goal.

They were tussling back and forth on top of the guns, each of them trying to grab for one and hold off his adversary at the same time.

Finally Claud managed to close his hand on one of the pistols. Nathan tried to knock it from his grasp with a smash of his fist. Claud grimaced with pain, but kept his hold on the gun. Then he gave a hard twist of his body that threw Nathan to one side.

The metallic rasp of metal on metal, as Claud cocked the pistol, slashed into Nathan's waning consciousness like ice. Throwing out a burst of strength, he grabbed Claud's wrist and twisted the fist-held gun back against him.

The pistol went off like thunder between the two men.

Claud's throat erupted a geyser of blood. His hand was still locked around the Colt as he slumped backward, his eyes rolling in a dying reflex.

Nathan groped for the other pistol and found it. He climbed laboriously to his feet, fumbling for balance.

Lolly was tough and wiry. Struggling with Snake, she'd succeeded in holding her own for a half minute. Then Snake tore the rifle from her hands and, rearing back, smashed the butt across her temple.

Even as Lolly slipped to the ground, Snake came wheeling around. He brought his gun to bear on Nathan, who was just getting to his feet.

Both men fired at the same time.

Nathan felt the knifing pain in his head. He staggered backward and nearly fell. Then he blinked his eyes clear. Snake Purley had gone down. Rolling about on the ground, writhing and groaning, he was clutching his right arm.

Taking a step toward him, Nathan again stumbled and almost fell. Half-reeling, he clamped a hand to his bleeding head and stood with legs braced apart. Lolly was getting unsteadily to her feet, dazedly shaking her head. A strawberry mark of mashed skin stood out sharply on her temple. She pressed a hand over it and winced, then looked blindly at the Purleys on the ground, two of them silent and unmoving. Her gaze passed on to Nathan.

"God," she said in a shaking voice. "You are bleeding like hell, Nate. There's blood all over you."

"I reckon most of it's Claud's." A woolly dullness seemed to clog his thoughts and his tongue. "I think I am hurt pretty bad, Lolly. We got to get away from here. Mostly it will be up to you."

CHAPTER 14

Cutting almost straight north and south, the awesome slash of Piegan Canyon formed much of Swallowtail's west boundary. It was hundreds of feet deep, so narrow that for miles sunlight never reached the bottom except at noon when the sun was overhead. There was greenery on the floor of the gorge, thick mottes of good-sized trees nourished by little streams and pools from springs higher up in the canyon and small feeder canyons that branched off it. All of it looked very pretty from up above.

But what had fascinated Ty Banner from child-hood was the vaulting sweep of Piegan Canyon's upper walls. When the sun struck the limestone and sandstone cliffs at particular angles during the day, the stains of erosion and the streaks of iron and salt in the rock created a spectacular mosaic of color.

Ty's big passion as an artist was for doing intimate studies of people at work or rest or play. But he'd long nursed the idea of doing a full-scale canvas in oils of Piegan Canyon, one that would capture all its marvelous detail of glowing rock with a photographic fidelity, only in color.

It would be quite a challenge. That's why he hadn't considered undertaking it until now—his first sober and optimistic day in a long, long while.

Halting his wagon a ways back from the canyon rim, Ty crutched his way over to the edge and sat down with pencil and crayons and sketch pad. For several hours he worked industriously at different concepts of his projected work. Now and then he hauled himself up on his crutches and worked up or down the rimrock, trying to size up the most advantageous angles.

For Ty, his art was his life—so far as life had any meaning for him outside of Serena. Today, since he was clear-headed and fully absorbed in his work, time passed quickly. He forgot about everything else, even the buried craving for liquor, until about noon. Then, when the first familiar rat-gnawings of his addiction began to have their way with him, he ate the sandwiches Serena had put up for him. They filled his belly and temporarily settled his desire for drink. Afterward he was able to stretch out in the sun, hat tipped over his eyes, and nap for a while.

Just one thing bothered him. That was the sense of being watched.

Ty couldn't explain it, but had felt it more than once even while absorbed in his preliminary sketches through the morning. The feeling of being spied on. More than once he'd jerked abruptly around, hoping to catch sight of whoever or whatever was the author of his discomfort.

But he'd seen nothing. The flats this side of the

canyon were sparsely laced with brush and might provide cover for any watcher. Only why the hell would anyone be watching *him?*

Spooked over nothing, Ty told himself. But the jittery feeling persisted. Maybe it was a sort of delusion: the kind a man built up in his mind to mask something else. Such as the wish for a slug of whiskey . . .

Ty ground his teeth. *No, goddammit!* He had to kill it. Kill it for good. Yet gradually, insidiously, as his after-eating torpor wore off, the tendrils of craving crept like nerves of fire through his brains and body.

I have to beat it, he thought grimly. *It's now or never.*

He picked up his work materials, heaved up on his crutch, trudged back to the canyon rim and sat down. It was an interesting view. Here the rimrock slanted downward at an easy, only slightly out-of-horizontal angle for maybe a hundred yards. Then it dropped off in an abrupt vertical plunge. That first hundred-yard slant gave an open, sweeping view of the canyon's opposite wall, whose rim soared fifty feet above the level of this side.

Ty tried to busy himself with more sketches, but the first freshness of the work had worn off. His best hours had always been in the morning; he tended to go stale as the day went on. Maybe it was that trickle of drab letdown as any day drew out its length that, several years ago, had first turned him to the bottle for a solution.

And the wish for whiskey was increasing in the back of his mind. *God!* Could he stand it much longer?

Ty swung to his feet and stared into the gulf of the canyon without really seeing it now. It would be so damned easy to drive to town and get stinking drunk. And to obtain a new supply of liquor at the same time.

On the edge of decision, wavering, he thought savagely: *No!*

Into his mind, with a sudden yearning pang, sprang the image of Serena. She was his mainstay. Just having her beside him could help. He'd forgotten that for a long time and had learned it all over again, last night. Sexual attraction. There was that, always. But there was a lot more, too.

Serena might not have a lot of strength of her own, but she was his strength, if he had any at all. Because he loved her. And that was the strongest feeling a man could know in a lifetime.

Decisively now, Ty got up and limped back to the buckboard. He stowed his sketching materials and his crutches in the wagon bed and then, wincing at the odd needles of pain that shot into his legs, hoisted himself up on the seat.

He would go home to Serena. And then they would talk. It had been a long time since they'd really talked together. If they were going to make any lasting change in their lives, they needed to thrash out a course of action that made sense to both. Ty was no cattleman. Never would be. He was an artist, heart and soul. Serena knew it too, as shown by her careful salvaging of work he had mutilated and thrown away in various fits of anger.

But where would they go from here? That's what Ty needed to know. The veering of his thoughts in that direction somewhat dulled the need for a drink. Suddenly he wanted only to be with his wife, to draw on the sensitivity of her private thoughts. Together, hopefully, the two of them might be able to reach some firm decisions.

Ty picked up the reins and clucked to the team, feeling a disgusted wave of remorse for his neglect of them through half a day. Once he'd settled into his sketching, he'd forgotten all about them. As soon as they got back to Swallowtail headquarters, he would see to tending their needs himself.

As Ty started to turn the wagon back toward the ranch road, Sixto Larraldes rode out of a nearby clot of brush. Caught by surprise, Ty pulled up the team. "Whoa!" he shouted. "Whoa!"

"*Buenas tardes*, Señor Banner."

Larraldes was broadly smiling. Generally he was a man who looked so sour that you wondered if his mother had bitten a pickle when he was born. Ty gave him a guarded nod, wondering what the hell Larraldes was doing here. This reach of Swallowtail range was far to the south of the line shack that had been held down by Larraldes and Pinky Miller since the Purleys had been discharged.

"Same to you," said Ty. "You've got a little bit off your stamping grounds, haven't you?"

"Ah. Yes. But there is good reason, eh?"

Still widely smiling, Larraldes reined over beside the buckboard. He was idly uncoiling a metal-tipped quirt in his hands. "The reason, Señor, is this—"

Suddenly the quirt lashed out and struck the rump of Ty's left-hand team horse. The animal squealed and lunged forward into its harness.

"Jesus Christ!" yelled Ty. "What are you doing? Whoa!"

Larraldes slashed the horse's rump again. It veered sideways, dragging its teammate with it. The animals veered as one in the direction of the canyon rim. Then, as Larraldes' quirt fell again, they broke into a panicked run.

The horses were wholly out of control now. Racing in a headlong rush for the rimrock where the long slow incline began and then, a hundred yards on, ended on a vertical drop to the canyon bottom.

Larraldes raced his mount alongside the team, pealing out crazy laughter as he lashed at the horses. Dimly, Ty thought he heard a gunshot and then another from somewhere behind. But that impression was overridden by a cold grip of terror as he fought for control of the team. The terrified horses plunged over the inclined rim and bolted down the long slant toward the sheer drop beyond.

Desperately Ty flung himself sideways, intending to throw himself off the wagon seat. Larraldes was ready for that. He slowed his own run enough to fall abreast of Ty, and then yanked his carbine from its saddle boot. He took a savage swing at Ty's head.

The muzzle caught him a glancing blow on the forehead. Stunned, Ty slumped downward on the seat. He was hardly aware of what happened next. He heard the crash of another gunshot, much closer this time. The team and wagon hurtled on toward the brink of the drop-off. And then they were turning sideways and slowing down. Someone was yelling, "*Alto*! *Alto*!"

Gradually the wagon was pulled to a dead stop.

Ty pulled himself upright with difficulty, shaking his head to clear it, blinking the spots out of his vision. He saw Sandal Cruz sitting a prancing pony and gripping the headstall of the right-hand team horse, saying soothing words to the animals. Like his grandfather, like Nate Drew, Sandal had an incredible touch with horses. Already they were calming down.

"What the hell?" Ty said dazedly.

"I am sorry, Señor Ty," said Sandal. "I almos' didn' get Larraldes in time. So you almos' die."

Ty swallowed and nodded. He could see as much for himself. Sandal had succeeded in turning the team, then bringing it to a stop on the slope about sixty feet from the vertical drop. Now, turning his head to look upslope, Ty saw Larraldes sprawled on his back, arms outflung, a dark shape against the dun earth. Larraldes' horse was standing a little way off.

"Is he . . . ?"

"Señor, I think he's dead as a man can be."

Sandal's lips barely moved on the words; his voice was trembling.

"Easy," said Ty. "Take it easy, boy."

Ty picked up his crutches and prepared to swing down to the ground. Sandal quickly dismounted from the pony and came over to assist him.

"Thanks," said Ty, once his feet were planted on solid ground and he could get his own shakes somewhat under control. "Now will you kindly tell me what the hell all this is about?"

In just a few minutes a whole lot of things were made clear to Ty Banner. So many of them at one time that all at once his legs felt even wobblier than usual. He had to sit down on the sloping ground and run his frantic thoughts back over what Sandal had told him.

Sandal's grandfather, it seemed, was familiar with the Larraldes family from many years back, down in Sonora. They were a *mucho mal* lot of people; their badness was bred in the blood. Sixto was the worst of them all. Even as a boy he had exhibited all the arrogant, bloodthirsty traits of a born *cabrón*. Later, in Arizona and New Mexico, he had taken up with outlaw gangs. When merely robbing banks and trains had proved too tame for him, Sixto had become a "warrior," a hired assassin, in cattle wars. After his involvement in the Chisum-Murphy feud in New Mexico, things had become so hot for him that he'd dropped quietly out of sight for a long time.

But his history was well-known to Sandal's grandfather. Diego Cruz had kept a close eye on the activities of Sixto and his partner, Pinky Miller, ever since Thorp Banner had hired them onto the Swallowtail crew not long ago.

It had seemed peculiar to old Diego that Larraldes had remained at headquarters after bringing in the body of Ike Banner. Why would Thorp Banner keep Sixto there rather than order him back to line-shack duty? Diego Cruz had sharpened his watch on Larraldes, and had confided his reasons to his grandson.

After Ty had ridden out this morning, Diego and Sandal had seen Thorp go to the bunkhouse. And shortly thereafter, Sixto had ridden out on

215

the ranch road where Ty had gone. *Quién sabe*? Perhaps it meant nothing. But Diego, taking no chances with one he knew to be a killer for hire, had instructed Sandal to follow Sixto Larraldes, to keep him in sight without being seen, and to take such action as his good sense told him the situation might require.

"Tha's what I do, Señor Ty," said Sandal. He looked quite sick; he gulped now and then as he talked. "You come here and this Sixto Larraldes follow you, and I follow him. All day long while you are drawing pictures, he is sit' back in the brush, jus' watching. Taking his time, I think."

"Why," Ty asked angrily and impatiently, "didn't you just come over and tell me what was up?"

"Would you believe any of it, Señor? Would you believe your own brother send this Larraldes to kill you?"

"I—" Ty paused, rubbing his aching forehead. He shook his head wearily, feeling as sick as Sandal looked. "No. Guess I wouldn't."

"That is it. You see? I could do nothing, then. What had this Larraldes done? He follow you and spy on you from the brush, that is all. That is nothing. So, I mus' wait and spy on him till he try something. That is what I do."

Ty gave a dull nod, looking at the pistol shoved in Sandal's belt. It was an old Whitneyville

Walker Colt with most of the bluing worn off the long barrel. "You got him with that, huh? That old cap-and-ball gun."

"*Si.* Is all *Abuelito* had to give me. Is old gun he have for many years. He clean it and load it up for me and tell me to take it along when I follow this Larraldes. *Abuelito*, he's so old he can't get on horse anymore. So I must do the thing."

Sandal broke off, swallowing hard against his queasiness. "So. I am to shoot Larraldes if I got to. If he make like to shoot you, I am to shoot him. But I am not expect what he try. All I can do, after he ride out and whip your horses, is I shoot at him fast. I miss. He take a shot at me and then go back to whipping team. I ride after him an' get close. Then I don' miss."

Sandal's young voice was starting to break. "I . . . I have killed a man! But I had to, Señor Ty! What could I do?"

"What you did," Ty said quietly. "Help me up, Sandal, will you?"

He stretched out his hand and Sandal grasped it. With the additional aid of a crutch, Ty swung to his feet.

"Do we go to the sheriff, Señor?"

"No," Ty said in the same quiet, remote voice. He felt almost dead to feeling. "We're going home. There are things I need explained to me, and Thorp is going to explain them. Whether he wants to or not. Sandal . . . go and collect Larraldes' guns, will you? Rifle and pistol both. His cartridge belt too. Could be I'll have need of them."

It was late in the afternoon when they reached Swallowtail headquarters. And Ty sensed it at once: a distinctly wrong feel about the place. It seemed unnaturally quiet and deserted. By this hour at least some of the crew should be coming in from their on-range duties.

Yet there wasn't a soul about as Ty pulled the buckboard to a stop by the corrals. With Sandal's help he swung to the ground. Damned strange . . . not even Diego Cruz or Jim Obie seemed to be around.

"Where the hell is everyone?" Ty wondered aloud.

"I don' know, Señor *Abuelito*, maybe he is over in the cabin we live in."

The front door of the main house opened. Diego Cruz came out and tramped slowly down the slope toward them. His brown face was set like seamed and wrinkled iron. He walked like a man who bore more than a weight of years on his shoulders.

"I have a thing to say to you, Señor," he said, and looked at his grandson. "It's not for your ears. Put up the wagon and tend the horses."

Sandal broke into a torrent of Spanish. All Ty could extract from any of it was that he was telling Diego that he had been forced to kill Sixto

Larraldes. Diego's face softened; he patted Sandal on the shoulder.

"*De nada*. That one was meant for a bad end. But it's bad for you to know you had to do the work. Later we will talk of it. Now I have a thing to tell Señor Banner."

As Sandal moved off to do his grandfather's bidding, Ty said impatiently, "For God's sake, what is it?"

"Is ver' bad. Is your wife, Señor."

Ty's flesh began to crawl even before Diego told him what had happened. Or at least as much as he knew.

A little while ago Celestina had come home from a visit to her relatives. She had found Mrs. Banner in a very bad condition. The housekeeper had been half-hysterical when she came seeking Diego Cruz. There was nobody else at the head-quarters to whom she might turn. But there was nothing that Diego could do in this situation. What had been done was done. He was not sure of all that had happened. Mrs. Banner was in a state of near-shock. Diego could get very little out of her except that she had been attacked by her brother-in-law.

By Thorp.

Ty hardly heard Diego's last words. He was crutching furiously toward the house. He hobbled through the front rooms and into the bedroom wing.

Serena was lying in their bed, under a blanket that was drawn up to her chin. Her blue eyes looked straight at the ceiling, blankly. Her left cheek was discolored by a great ugly bruise. Celestina, who was bending over her, moved aside as Ty came to the bedside. He dropped his crutches and fell on his knees, ignoring the stab of pain in his legs.

"See. Oh my God. See . . ."

For a moment there was no reaction at all from her. Then she turned her head slowly to look at him. She tried to smile. "Ty," she whispered.

"What, darling? What happened?"

She turned her face away from him.

Ty looked at Celestina. *"What?"* he demanded fiercely. "Damn it, woman! Speak up!"

The housekeeper wrung her fat hands. "I . . . I'm not sure, Señor. Your brother did it. I come home and I find her on the floor. She has no clothes on. She . . . she has been beaten. I think your brother . . . I think he use her as a man uses a woman. She could not tell me much."

Ty's brain was numb with shock. But it was functioning well enough for him to piece things together in a purely mechanical way.

Thorp. He had arranged for Larraldes to kill Ty and make it seem an accident. Ty's team would have gone out of control and carried him and the buckboard to a shattering death at the bottom of Piegan Canyon. That was what searchers, finding the broken bodies of Ty and the horses and the wreckage of the buckboard, would have to assume.

Afterward, apparently on a whim of uncontrollable lust, Thorp had raped and beaten Serena.

About the rest of it, Ty did not have to guess. Old Diego could tell him exactly what happened. Thorp had ordered the ranch hands in from their range duties and told them he had evidence that people at Lynchtown were responsible for Ike Banner's death. He intended to wipe that scurvy pesthole of squatters out this same night, and he wanted to know how many of the crew would ride with him. Except for Diego Cruz, they had volunteered to a man.

They had ridden out in a body for Lynchtown. More than a dozen of them. Only Diego Cruz had remained behind. A little later Celestina had returned to find Serena in a terrible condition.

That was not all of it, of course. There had to be more, perhaps more than a man could even guess at . . . or want to guess at. His mind could take in only so much at one time. Ty knew enough. Enough to know what he was going to do. To Thorp. And maybe to Freeman, too. Thorp had sent Free to town on some errand, and he'd returned shortly before Thorp and the crew had departed; Free had gone with them. Of course

Free was Thorp's unquestioning satellite, but he might or might not be deeply involved in whatever intrigues Thorp had underway.

I'll find out, thought Ty.

He told Diego Cruz what must be done now. Sandal must be sent to town to get a doctor for Serena. Meantime he, Ty, was going after Thorp and the others. A lot of questions remained to be answered. And Thorp had better come up with some damned good answers.

Including what had happened to Nathan Drew.

Diego said no word of objection. One look at Ty's face must have shown him the futility of argument. He said merely, "I don' think you get ver' far on a wagon going to Lynchtown, Señor. She is some ver' rough country back there."

"No wagon," Ty said quietly. "I'm taking a saddle horse. Rig one up for me, Diego."

"But Señor. Your legs—"

"I'll keep on the horse all right. You saddle one up. Just see it has a rifle boot on it."

Larraldes' shell belt and pistol were cinched around Ty's waist. He had Larraldes' Winchester too. The supply of .44 cartridges in the shell belt would fit either weapon.

"Señor. What I mean, here I can help you on the horse. If you fall off, how will you get back on?"

Ty's lips tugged into the painful semblance of a grin. "Why, that's easy. You get a rope and run it

222

under the horse's barrel. You tie the ends to my legs and pull it tight as you can and make it fast. No way I can fall off. Is there?"

"No. Is no way you can get away from horse then," Diego said carefully. "Also, if you slip off the saddle, you will roll underneath him. Then you will get drag' to death."

Ty was already nodding his head, still grinning a little. "That did occur to me. Get me a horse and saddle him, Mr. Cruz. And get that piece of rope, will you?"

CHAPTER 15

Snake's bullet had ripped a furrow through Nathan's scalp. By steeling himself against the pain, he could run a finger along it and feel the bared bone. There was little bleeding, but somehow it must be worse than it seemed. Maybe the chunk of lead had glanced from his head at a slight angle. Whatever the reason, he was dizzy and stumbling afterward. He couldn't even manage to brace his legs under him without Lolly's help.

She wasn't angry with him anymore. Sobered by what had happened, all Lolly cared about now was doing the best she could for him. Nathan had told her as much as he knew of the situation, and Lolly proceeded in a businesslike way to do all that had to be done.

Nathan's scalp wasn't bleeding much. To temporarily stop the blood flow, Lolly hunted for and found a sack of flour in the cabin. She plastered a handful of flour over the wound. It quickly soaked up and coagulated the blood.

Claud and Sheb Purley were stone dead. Snake was only slightly wounded. Going in at close range, the .45 slug had torn his right arm up some. Fired just an instant before Snake's gun went off, it had likely broken Snake's aim enough to keep Nathan from being shot dead center.

While Snake was still rolling around clutching his arm, Lolly managed to get a rope around him and tie him up fast. She also did a hasty job of bandaging his arm. Then she dragged him into the cabin and left him on the floor. She told Nathan that she wasn't minded to do anything more for "this damned old devil," and that much was more than he deserved.

Nathan agreed with her. But he was hardly in shape to say even that much. His horse was in the makeshift aspen-pole corral the Purleys had rigged up behind the cabin. Lolly bridled and saddled the piebald and helped him climb aboard. He was able to stay in leather by gripping the saddle horn and clamping the horse's barrel with his legs, and putting every shred of his remaining consciousness into holding himself erect. Being in sorry shape already from the Purleys' treatment of him, he had few resources left on which to draw.

"Don't know how far I can make it," he whispered. "Going to be touch and go, Lolly. All I know, we can't stay here. Thorp will be coming back soon . . ."

"I know, Nate. You told me. All right now, just listen. I am going to get you to Lynchtown. Ain't a person, saving maybe my brother Adakhai, who won't do what needs to be done to help you. Understand what I'm saying? . . . *Nate!*"

She was gripping his rein and gazing up at him

fierce-eyed. Nathan raised his chin off his chest and managed to bob his head, once. "Sure, Lolly. But Lynchtown's like to be where Thorp will look for me first of all. I don't want to draw lightning on 'em."

"Seems to me we'll draw plenty of that anyway, with old Ike gone," she said grimly. "That Thorp . . . he's a pure-quill bad one. What little I ever seen of him, I always thought so. Some brothers you got. Now hear me. You have *got* to hold yourself in that saddle as far as Lynchtown. Try!"

Nathan nodded again, woozily.

She was right. No matter where else they headed, he wouldn't get far in his condition. Thorp would cover these hills with trackers and eventually they would find him. With Ike dead, the people of Lynchtown would have to fight to protect their own, and they would fight for him too. That was his best chance now.

He had only patchy impressions of what happened over the next few hours. On foot and leading his horse, Lolly struck out east across woods and meadow and up the pine-covered ridge where her own camp was hidden. Here she swiftly threw her gear together and diamond-hitched it on her packhorse, then ran a line from its bridle to Nathan's saddle horn. She ran another from Nathan's bridle to her saddle pony. Afterward she mounted and was on the move again, still eastward and leading Nathan's piebald.

His head sank down to his chest. He held his legs fast against the horse's barrel. And he kept something like a deathgrip on his saddle horn.

Hours went by. Nathan knew that much because the light washed steadily out of the sky. It flattened to a narrow lemon band in the far west . . . and that too vanished. But the moon was nearly full. As its flow relieved the gray weave of dusk, Lolly picked her way unerringly across the high country meadows and pinewoods that she knew like the palm of her hand.

At some indistinct point in time, they approached the great cliff-bounded bowl of land that cupped Lynchtown. They knew when they were drawing near it by the fan of ruddy light flung up by the village fires. It limned the rimrock of surrounding cliffs in black relief. Nathan and Lolly emerged from a stretch of woods toward the northerly rim, and now they would have to work around it and then downward to the valley entrance.

Suddenly Lolly reined up close to the rimrock, staring down into the valley. When he felt his horse pulled to a stop, Nathan blinked his eyes to a hazy alertness.

"What is it?"

"Something ain't right down there," Lolly said tersely. "Something—"

She swung to the ground and got the field

glasses out of her saddlebag and moved close to the rim. She dropped to one knee and trained the glasses on the scene below. Nathan floundered out of his saddle, keeping himself upright by not letting go the saddle horn till he was sure he had his legs under him. His steps were slow and shaky as he went over to Lolly and settled on his haunches beside her.

Something funny was going on, all right. All the men of the village were out, it looked like. They were drawn up in a rambling line facing a bunched group of horsemen, and some of them were carrying torches. That illuminance, along with the light of scattered cooking fires, picked out details of the tableau with a raw, flickering intensity.

"Damn!" Lolly muttered. "It's *him* . . . that rotten brother of yours!"

"Give me those—"

Not waiting for her response, he took the binoculars roughly from Lolly's hands and set them to his eyes. For a moment the scene was a fiery blur; then it swam to focus. He passed the glasses across the crowd of villagers to verify his first impression. These were all men, all of them armed to the teeth, all tensely waiting.

Jack Lynch stood out ahead of the others, tall and unbent as he faced the riders, who'd obviously just entered through the cleft at the valley's south end. Nathan swung the glasses, trying to catch the leader of the horsemen in his sights. He was sitting his horse a little way out from his companions, hands crossed on his pommel. Nathan caught his face in the glasses and steadied on it.

Yes. It was Thorp.

Things hadn't gone quite as Thorp Banner had expected.

He'd figured that a night raid on Lynchtown would catch its inhabitants off guard. But even as he and his men had neared the gorge that gave ingress to the Lynchtown valley, a single rifle shot had echoed in the night.

It was fired, of course, by a sentry stationed on the rimrock of the gorge. Plainly it was intended as a warning signal. Maybe the Lynchtowners had gotten word, somehow, of Ike Banner's death. Or they were just on the alert because they feared they'd be blamed for the recent rash of cattle stealing, even if Ike had first been apprised of it through Jack Lynch.

Whatever the case, they were ready.

Coming in by night, Thorp and his crew were quite close before the sentry spotted them. But his warning shot came soon enough for the Lynchtown men to turn out in force, standing in a wide-flung line near the mouth of the valley as the Swallowtail crew came thundering in. The Lynchtowners were armed with everything from bows and arrows to Green River knives and old trade muskets.

They looked ready to die on the spot if they had to. All of them did.

That sobering realization put a check on Thorp's rage to send the whole shebang to hell-and-gone in one spectacular raid and then drive any survivors off Swallowtail range. He pulled his mount to a halt and raised his hand, bringing his men to a stop behind him.

Jack Lynch stood in front of the other Lynchtowners. Now he came slowly forward till he was a few yards from Thorp. "There now, Mr. Banner," he said quietly. "Ye may see it will not be as easy a business as you'd counted on. We can both of us die right here and now, you and me. And a lot of others too. But is it worth it?"

Thorp bared his teeth in a great wolfish grin. "That's up to you, old fella. Maybe you didn't know my pa is dead."

He had the satisfaction of seeing Jack Lynch's expression break a little. But just as quickly, it hardened again.

"I did not," said Jack Lynch. "I'm sorry for it. But it don't change what is. I've my people to think of. This is our place, Thorp Banner. We've lived on the spot an a'mighty lot of years. There is no law or written paper can change that. If ye've come to roust us out, as I take it you have . . . why boy, I can certify you will be taking underholts on a wildcat."

"M'm. Could be." Thorp rubbed his chin, thoughtfully. "I tell you what. You folks can pack up and move out o' here. Now. Tonight. Or like you suggest, there can be a lot o' dying right on this spot. But there don't need to be."

"That says nothing I didn't say."

"You leave me finish, now." Thorp leaned forward and settled his crossed hands on his pommel, grinning just a little. "Reason there don't need to be, I can pull back out o' here with my men and there won't be no shooting right away. Only after that, what I will do is, I will round up every white man I can from every goddamn ranch in this county. Ain't none of 'em happy about this scab you call Lynchtown, old squawman. Now Pa's gone, they will be honing to help me wipe it out. Ought to round me up a few hunderd of 'em with no trouble. And 'fore they are done, they will make a godawful mess of you and yours. What you think of that?"

Jack Lynch did not reply. But a flicker of indecision showed in his seamed face before he stoically masked it.

"Another thing," Thorp added casually. "There's all them squaws and brats of yours. I take it they are hid back in them lodges yonder. Well, leave me tell you, old fella, once we have mopped up their menfolk—and you can lay odds we will—

we will go ahead and clean out all them squaws same way. Nits make lice. What I am sort of saying, if you and your bucks don't care that much 'bout your own hides, maybe you care some'at 'bout how your squaws and brats fare. Huh?"

Thorp was partly bluffing. Not all that many whites would have stomach for the full-scale retribution he was suggesting. But if he made out as though he believed it, maybe Jack Lynch—an exile from his own race for so many years— would believe it too.

Jack Lynch's expression did not change. But Thorp noted a perceptible sag of his shoulders, a fleeting token of defeat and resignation.

That suited Thorp—for now. He had every intention of following through on his plan to shut Jack Lynch's mouth for good. But it would have to wait. If he and his crew had succeeded in taking the village by surprise, though, Jack Lynch could have been shot down in the confusion. Thorp could have done it himself, and nobody the wiser as to the deliberation behind the act.

He would figure out another way, that was all. Right now, it evidently suited Jack Lynch to declare nothing about whatever he knew of Ike's last wishes and his deposition. Nor would he say anything else that might legally militate against Thorp in the courts. Probably he would bide his time, knowing the futility of challenging Thorp here and now. He'd mean to do so later. But before then, Thorp silently vowed, he would be dead.

"All right, you bloody spalpeen," Jack Lynch said quietly. "They'll go as I say they should. But I'll not say a death sentence on 'em. So ye win. What is it you want, if you'll be so kind as to spell it to a detail?"

"Real easy," said Thorp. "What you do, you and them other bucks, is you walk over one at a time and throw your weapons on that big blaze yonder." He pointed at an overfed fire. "You shed all the hardware you got, each one o' you, right out where we can see it. Then I will give you enough time for you all to pack up your possibles and pack the hell out o' here."

"What comes then?" Jack Lynch asked in a strained voice.

"Why then this whole damn rat's nest of yours gets burned to hell up. Right down to ashes. Then we will give you an escort across the county line. You got all that?"

"I got enough."

For a long moment Jack Lynch stood as he was, slowly fisting and unfisting his hands. Then he turned to face the line of men and started to say something in one siwash tongue or another. Thorp couldn't follow the sense of it; he said sharply, "Old fella, I want to be damn sure what you are saying. So you say it over in good straight English, all right? I lay odds most of 'em know it even if they don't use it much."

Jack Lynch did not even look at Thorp. But he paused and then spoke again, now in English. His voice was quiet, yet firm and reaching. And it brought a reaction that Thorp hadn't looked for.

All the Lynchtown men stood motionless and listening. Except one. A lean youth who came running out from the line and threw a rifle to his shoulder, levering it and lining it on Thorp. For one shocked instant Thorp Banner looked into the cold muzzle of death and knew, in the same disbelieving moment, that nothing could head it off in time.

The thought came even as a shot crashed out. But it wasn't from the Indian's gun.

The youth was flung backward by the bullet's impact, yet somehow kept his feet. His rifle went off with his reflex tug on the trigger. But it discharged into the ground, for he was already falling forward. He arched over on his back in a single dying convulsion, then lay still.

For a moment everything seemed to hang suspended, like a grease drop in water. Nobody on either side moved. They all seemed frozen and undecided in the wake of sudden and unexpected death.

Thorp turned his head and saw that Free had

ranged up alongside him with a faint insolent grin, smoke wisping from the muzzle of his pistol. "Like I told you, big brother," Free said into the silence. "Ain't nothing gives a guy an edge like a good fast gun. Right now you like to be good and gone if it wasn't so. Hey?"

There was a sudden jerk of movement as Jack Lynch wheeled and started toward the fallen youth. Then he came to a dead stop. He clamped his hands to his chest and slowly turned, his face squeezed with pain. He toppled over in a kind of slow, measured fall, like that of a tree going down. And lay unmoving.

Christ! Thorp couldn't believe it for a moment. The old man's heart or something. Whatever, it was a stroke of luck for him.

All the men were still frozen in place, and Thorp seized advantage of the moment. He gigged his horse forward a yard or so, at the same time shooting his arm up and yelling, "All right now! That's enough. Been enough harm done. All I want is what I said before. You hear me?"

The first paralysis had broken. A ripple of stirrings ran through the Lynchtown men. But they only muttered among themselves and fingered their guns. That was all.

"Come on, now!" Thorp roared lustily. "Leave us be reasonable, all right? Ain't nobody else needs to get hurt. . . ."

For a few moments it still looked as if it might go either way. But the bulk of the Lynchtown men took Thorp seriously, and they had quick rough words for those who were undecided. In the end, every one of them walked over to the big fire and pitched his weapons into it. They did it slowly, one by one. The explosions of detonated cartridges and flares of ignited powder kept everyone's nerves keyed to an uneasy high.

But every damned one of them obeyed the order.

Afterward it was just a matter of herding the lot of them together and then rousting the women and kids out of the lodges. Thorp gave them time enough to gather their belongings and pile them on makeshift travois they could hitch behind their ponies. But he wouldn't permit them to round up their sheep and goats in the adjoining valley. He wanted the Lynchtowners to clear out fast, which couldn't be managed if they had to herd along a passel of animals. Besides, he wanted to drive home a final object lesson to them. So he gave his men orders to shoot all the damned woolies and goats in that valley and leave their carcasses to rot.

Matter of fact, Thorp could have meted out the same fate to the villagers themselves and not have been the least troubled by it. But his crew wouldn't have consented to go that far, and it would have made a hell of a stink if word leaked out. Anyway, no further violence should be necessary. He'd have this passel of scum off his land, and that was all that mattered.

His land, by God. Nobody else's.

The kid that Free had shot, it turned out, was Adakhai, a hothead grandson of Jack Lynch. As a result Jack Lynch had been seized by a stroke or something. It didn't matter what. The old man was just as dead.

An aged woman hobbled from the direction of the lodge and knelt down beside Jack Lynch's body. She stayed that way on her knees, giving out long keening moans. Turned out she'd been the old man's squaw. Thorp generously said it was all right for her to stay by him as long as she wanted. But the rest of the people had to clear out right away. His crew would give them an escort to the county line. . . .

Leaving a few of his men behind with orders to kill all the animals and fire the village, Thorp rode out ahead of the Lynchtowners, some mounted and some walking, flanked on all sides by the handful of Swallowtail crewmen. Jack Lynch's death seemed to have left them stunned, any spirit of resistance broken. It should be easy to herd them across Swallowtail land and over its nearest boundary. And they'd been given to understand that any attempt of theirs to return would damned well be fatal.

Thorp suppressed a chuckle. Things were breaking pretty well for him.

From back in the valley came the crackle of gunfire. And soon the light of the burning lodges made a leaping glow against the cobalt sky. Thorp's mind flickered back briefly, indifferently, to the look of unquenchable hatred on the face of Jack Lynch's squaw as she had ceased her bitter wailings long enough to stare straight at him.

He smiled and let the thought pass. Almost everything was sewed up now.

It hadn't been difficult to convince his crewmen that the Lynchtowners, at least some of them, were responsible for Ike's death. Thorp had explained that Nathan Drew had gone out to check on sign at the place where Sixto Larraldes had found Ike's body. He'd reported his findings back to Thorp, and what he'd found pointed to the probability that Lynchtown people were responsible for Ike's death and had tried to make it look like an accident. Indications were that Ike had caught some of them making off with Swallowtail cattle, and so they had killed him and had tried to make it appear an accident. As Thorp had told it to the crew, he'd then told Nathan to return to the spot and try to find more sign. Something that would pin down the exact circumstances of how Ike had met his end. Not that the crew needed any more persuading. To a man, they had volunteered to help him wipe out Lynchtown.

In the same vein, Thorp had directed Sixto Larraldes to rig Ty's death so it would seem accidental. As to his own attack on Serena, Thorp wasn't at all concerned about any possible consequences. See's terror of him would keep her mouth shut, and he'd reinforce that fear by a specific threat of what would happen if she didn't.

It still pleased him to muse on what he might do with Serena next. Marry her? To wed Ty's widow might help cinch his control of Swallowtail. Or he might just keep her around. Either way, he could do whatever he liked with Serena. Terrified and totally submissive, she would be an ideal plaything for a man like him. That was how Thorp liked a woman to be. There would be plenty of time to decide what he wanted to do with her.

Meantime, Free had visited their shyster lawyer in town and had had him draw up a proper quitclaim deed. It crackled in the side pocket of Thorp's coat as he brought a hand up and patted it. Yessir. Just about everything was sewed up. Except for a few dangling threads. The main one was Nate Drew.

Thorp was impatient to tie up every loose end and have done with it. Just maybe, he thought, that could be managed with no delay at all.

He looked at Free riding alongside him and said quietly, "Tell you what, little brother. If you are game, we best not wait to wrap ever'thing up for us. Not if we can get it all done right away."

Free looked at him in a puzzled way, but promptly nodded. "Sure, big brother. Whatever you say."

CHAPTER 16

When Lolly saw Adakhai shot down, she was paralyzed with disbelief. Then she saw Jack Lynch, too, collapse to the ground. With a moan she let the field glasses slip from her nerveless fingers.

"Oh God. They've killed my brother. Grandpa . . ."

Nathan's eyes were blurring again; he could barely make out what was going on. But the sound of that gunshot from below roused him. "What?" he said thickly. "Lolly—"

But she was already lunging to her feet, running to her mount and wrenching her rifle free of its boot. She came stumbling back and dropped on her stomach by the rim. Then levered the rifle and began to take aim. Nathan slapped his hand on the barrel and pinned it against the ground.

"Are you crazy?"

"I'm going to kill those sons-of-bitching brothers of yours!"

"Not this way you won't—"

"Damn you!" She tried to yank the weapon from his grasp, and when she couldn't, swung a doubled fist at his chin.

Catching the blow on his temple sent a blaze of pain through Nathan's throbbing head. He almost passed out from the shuddering agony of it. His response was prompt and instinctive. He pulled back his free hand, formed a fist and slammed Lolly in the jaw with all his remaining strength.

She went limp beside him. Fighting to hold onto consciousness, Nathan picked up the rifle and field glasses and moved a few yards off from her. Then he fixed the glasses on what was happening below.

He could hear Thorp bawling orders. The villagers were coming together in a tight group, flanked by some of the Swallowtail men. They headed out of the valley, Thorp and Free riding ahead. After that things went murky again for Nathan, but he had enough left to be aware that a few crewmen left behind were firing the lodges. And a rattle of gunfire from the adjoining valley indicated that the Lynchtown animals, exclusive of the ponies that the villagers had taken along, were being finished off.

He'll pay for this, Nathan thought obscurely, his mind full of Thorp and his pure callousness. But it was a sluggish reflex of a thought, almost without meaning in the soggy drift of his brain.

Lolly groaned and rolled to a sitting position. She looked at Nathan, sitting close by, her rifle across his knees.

She eyed him almost with hatred. "I could of

got 'em. I could of got 'em both. But blood's thicker than water, eh?"

"Don't be a fool," Nathan said wearily. "I could have shot them as easy as you could. But not at this distance. Not by firelight and not shooting way down at an angle."

"Damn you," Lolly said in a dazed, bitter voice. She passed a hand tenderly over her jaw as she stared down at the flaming lodges. "I could of got 'em, damn you. And now they're gone. Where is everybody?"

Nathan told her.

Lolly rose unsteadily to her feet. "Give me my gun."

He stirred his head back and forth, tiredly. "I'll hang onto it a spell. No telling what you might be minded to try. Lolly, if you'd shot at Thorp or Free, hit 'em or not, you'd have brought the whole crew swarming up here in nothing flat. And I'm in no fit way to fight or run right now."

She glared at him, touching her jaw. "You done good enough. Go to hell, Nate Drew."

Without another word she turned and tramped away along the rim. Nathan watched her go, feeling the dregs of his strength going too. He knew she was going down to the village, and that was all right. The handful of men Thorp had left behind had done their dirty work and had ridden away.

Nathan dropped back full length on the ground. The moon and stars pinwheeled in his fading vision against the blackness overhead. And then there was only the blackness.

He was awakened by a hand shaking his shoulder. It was Lolly, kneeling beside him. She said tonelessly, "Can you get up?"

With her help he eased up onto his haunches and then to his feet. He must have been out for several hours, anyway. The first gray hint of false dawn was tinging the sky. It gave just enough light for him to make out Lolly's face. Her expression was dead to feeling. Her eyes were black and stony, and if she'd shed any tears, he could see no sign of them.

"I can keep on my feet, I reckon."

"You just worry about keeping on a horse. That's what you'll have to do for a spell. There's a place I know of that I'm taking you to. It's anyway a three-four hour ride."

"All right."

Nathan's tongue was dry and furry; he could hardly form words. When he took a step, he nearly fell on his face. But Lolly was at his side, supporting him, and with her aid he managed to get astride his horse.

The next hours were a repetition of the slogging journey of late yesterday. Lolly riding ahead, heading up his horse and her pack animal, while Nathan put everything he had into holding his saddle.

The false dawn faded to a glory of sunrise that sent a chaos of splintery light against his reeling brain. They rode across lush meadows and through the twilight gloom of tall pine groves. He had no idea of where she was taking him and did not care.

Time lost all meaning. But later on he would figure it was something like mid-morning when Lolly called a halt. She helped him off his horse and got him into the looming shade of a rock wall. She made up a pallet of blankets and rolled him onto it.

Nathan knew that much. And then he knew nothing.

He slept through the day and woke late that night. A few yards away a small fire was crumbling to ripe coals. Lolly was curled up beside it in her blankets, fast asleep. He could hear a gurgle of water and see its rushing glimmer out beyond the rim of firelight, so they were close to a fast-running river or creek. He made out a black outline of cliffs against a lesser darkness of sky above. They were in a place that was well-hidden, or Lolly wouldn't risk a fire.

That was all Nathan could tell for sure, because the firelight that stressed the immediate scene also emphasized the outside darkness, and besides he was still fearfully drowsy. The reeling dizziness seemed to have partly passed. But he was conscious of a burning thirst. He was steeling himself to get up and look for water when he saw the canteen Lolly had left within arm's reach of him.

Nathan drank his fill and felt better. But he hadn't the least wish for food. And the desire to get more sleep was overwhelming. He lay back and within seconds was sleeping almost dreamlessly.

When he awoke once more, another dawn had come. It lay softly pink and gold on the cliff-cordoned valley. And now, clearheaded again, he at once recognized the place where they were. It was a snug pocket of open, well-grassed meadows that were broken by mottes of brush and trees, and it was located in the rugged foothills not far north of Lynchtown.

Nathan had camped here more than once on hunting or fishing sojourns when he wanted to get off by himself. With granite cliffs rearing on all sides, there was only one way to get into the valley by foot or on horseback: a narrow canyon at its western end. Outside of that, the only breaks in the surrounding walls were formed by the deep chasm of a river that had pounded for centuries through a narrow slot in the valley's north ramparts. At the broad bend where Lolly had made camp, the water ran swift and deep before it snaked crookedly through a cleft in the cliffs toward the south. He silently congratulated Lolly on her choice of a hiding place.

Gingerly Nathan edged to a sitting position and looked around. The fire was a mound of dead ashes. Lolly was nowhere to be seen. But she was around. Even if he couldn't see the three horses hobbled and grazing on a nearby stretch of meadow, he could hear sounds of splashing behind a shield of greenery that bordered the river. There was a small pile of clothes on the bank. Fed by ice-cold mountain streams, he supposed the river was just the place for a morning bath if a body went for that sort of thing.

Reckon I could use a clean-up myself, Nathan thought, rubbing a hand over his whiskered jaw. But I better sing out and let her know I am up and about. Matter of fact, he thought as he carefully rose to his feet, he felt pretty good. A touch of dizziness yet, but his head was clear and didn't hurt much. His scalp felt sort of funny, and putting a hand to his head he found a ridge of caked mash plastered along the wound. A Navajo poultice for sure: best thing in the world for drawing any infection and hastening the healing.

He'd opened his mouth to hail Lolly when she came into sight. The riverbank brush had concealed her, but a few steps to one side brought her into full view. Standing in the mid-thigh-deep water, she paused, arms lifted to slick back her dripping hair. For a moment she filled all his awareness: her wet skin gleaming smoky-bronze in the sun, the bold little cones of her breasts tilting up and out, her cap of short black hair glistening like a seal pelt.

Then she saw him. Surprise and anger rushed into her face. She splashed back behind cover, yelling, "Damn you, Nate Drew!"

Nathan didn't think she sounded as much shocked as hotly furious. He stood for an awkward, flat-footed moment, not knowing what to say. Finally he called, "Lolly?"

"What!"

"I'll turn my back and you come out and get dressed. All right?"

"All right, damn you!"

He turned and sat down facing the rock wall. He felt thirsty again, or maybe his mouth was just drier than it should be. Picking up the canteen, he took a long pull at it. His blood made a slugging pulse in his ears while he listened to little sounds made by Lolly as she emerged from the water and pulled on her clothes. Touch of fever, he supposed. Man couldn't just shrug off a bad scalp wound in a day and a couple nights.

Presently Lolly came up the slope and began fixing coffee, making an angry clatter as she dug into the pile of her gear. Not looking at him, she said coldly, "You hungry? Want something to eat?"

"Yes, thanks. Look, uh, I didn't mean to spy on you."

Lolly's mouth was compressed to a line as she dumped Triple X into the small battered coffee-pot, filled it with water from the canteen and set it next to the fire. With a stick she stirred up a few live coals and fed more sticks among them till she had a compact fire going. Then she finally met his gaze.

"Guess you didn't," she said, only a trifle less coldly. "I didn't mean to damn you, neither. Seems I been doing quite a lot of that. How you feeling?"

"Middling. A lot better than I did." He touched his scalp. "Is this the prickly pear poultice? That works about the best."

"Uh-huh." There was a visible thaw in her tone. "Thleen Chikeh showed me how to make it long time ago."

"What about her? What about Jack Lynch . . . and Adakhai?"

Lolly did not reply immediately. She began to knead flour and water together to form a ball of dough. And finally, slowly and quietly, she began to talk.

After leaving Nathan on the rim night before last, she had gone down to what was left of the village. All the lodges had been set afire. All the sheep and goats had been slaughtered. Only three people remained in Lynchtown and two of them were dead. Lolly had helped Thleen Chikeh, her grandmother, bury the bodies of her brother and grandfather.

And they had talked. Her grandmother had told Lolly all that she knew of the circumstances that had knit Jack Lynch and Ike Banner in a conspiracy of silence these many years. For the first time, Nathan was able to sort out the various facts concerning his own past. It all fit together. He was as much a son of Ike Banner as Thorp or Ty or Free . . . and maybe he had as strong a claim as any of them to Ike's legacy.

That was one thing, at least, of which Thorp had told him the cold truth.

Nathan thought back on the last few years, and of how things had come to be with Ike and him. There had been the deepening friendship, a warm and genuine thing for both men. But he couldn't have known how much deeper it must have run with Ike. Estranged in so many ways from his acknowledged sons, he'd increasingly sought the companionship of the son he could not acknowledge.

Only Ike himself could have given all the reasons behind his union with Horse Woman during his brief return to the Navajo band nearly three decades ago, and those reasons he had taken with him to the grave. Meantime there had been Luella. If the true story of Nathan's paternity had been revealed, it would have broken Luella's heart. So Ike had held silence for as long as she lived. After her death a few years ago, bringing out the truth would have been little more than a belated gesture. It would have stirred up a hornet's nest of complications that Ike, in his old age, had no taste for confronting. By that time his three legal sons were presenting him with enough problems. Why add to them?

No. You couldn't rightly blame Ike. He'd been a rawhide-tough man to the core, but direct and simple in his ways. He wasn't made for dealing with a lot of involved crap of that kind. So he'd quietly and simply shunted around it, and around his own burden of guilty feelings, by taking in and sheltering Horse Woman and her son and doing as well by them as he could under the circumstances. And later on, toward the end of his life, by coming to a (perhaps agonizing) conclusion that his "natural" son deserved a proper bequest. Even if it meant re-opening an old wound.

Ike would have wanted Lynchtown to survive his death. Knowing Thorp wouldn't permit it, he had willed that section of his range to Nathan. But the matter must have gone deeper yet. Even deeper, Nathan realized, than the blood tie between Ike and him. But too, Ike Banner's world had gone empty after Luella's death. At the last, his unacknowledged son had filled a lonely void.

And so each man had found a friend.

Lolly cooked up bacon and pan bread and a pot of strong black coffee. She and Nathan sat cross-legged facing one another, a little self-consciously, and ate hungrily. Nathan felt better with a solid meal under his belt.

Without looking up from her plate, Lolly said, "From what Grandma told me, Horse Woman hated ole Ike. And she hated you too. Her own son."

Nathan gave a slow, bleak nod. "I always knew it, Lolly. Never knew why . . . till now."

"I reckon she had good reason. Leastways by her way of looking at it."

"Sure. I can see that."

Lolly frowned, wiping crumbs from her lips. "Ain't easy for a body to say things like that, Nate. They just got to come out, same as proud flesh has got to be burned if you want to close it off. But it burns like hell. Don't it?"

Nathan twitched a suggestion of a smile. "Let's say it pinches a mite in the tight places. Look. There's something I want to tell you."

"Yeah? What's that?"

"Just thanks. Thanks for your help. After you left me on the rim, I didn't reckon you would come back. Wouldn't have blamed you if you didn't."

She gave him a brief, sharp glance. "Hell, I couldn't of just deserted you. Anyways . . . after I had this talk with Grandma, I knew what dirt had been done you. You sure got your share of it, Nate."

"That's another matter," Nathan said quietly. "What about Thleen Chikeh? What will happen with her?"

"I asked her. Said I would take care of her now and she said no." Lolly stirred her shoulders in a faint shrug. "Said she would follow her people where they go. Told me to get back to you and care for you and not think about her. That's how it is, Nate. You can't force yourself on a body."

She gave him another sharp look, but this one lingered on him. Her eyes met his as if questioning.

"I'm glad you came back, Lolly. Not just because you saved my neck, either."

"H'm." Lolly stared at her plate for a long moment. She gave him another brief, but dead serious look, then lowered her eyes again. "Listen, Nate. If we are going to say things straight out, it's time I was straight with you. I— well, I got a feeling for you. It goes pretty deep. Been that way since I was a little girl. It ain't changed a whit over the years. I don't reckon it ever will."

"Lolly—"

"Yeah, I know. I am only a kid as them things

are always reckoned. I am just going onto seventeen and you are getting to be sort of old."

Nathan almost smiled, but managed to keep his voice sober. "Twenty-eight. You call that old?"

"Well, yeah. I mean, by my lights, that's kind of old. But it don't change how I have always felt." Lolly wasn't quite able to hold back a smile of her own. This time she avoided his eyes by looking past his shoulder. "Damn it. I can't help it, Nate Drew. That's how it is."

"Lolly . . ."

"Yeah?"

"Look at it like this. When I am thirty, you'll be nineteen. When I'm forty, you'll be twenty-nine."

Her brows drew to a frown. "Jeez, I can figure that for myself! You making fun of me or what? Damn you, Nate Drew!"

"Look," Nathan said patiently. "Suppose you keep from ruffling up your feathers just one time. All I'm saying, the older a couple of people get, the less difference between 'em a few years are likely to make. Now, you get what I am trying to say?"

"I . . . hope I do. You mean it?"

"Lolly. Will you look straight at me for a while?"

She did.

"All right. Now I'll say it all. . . ."

CHAPTER 17

Ty Banner had gotten himself in a hell of a fix.

It had been late in the day when he had set out for Lynchtown and a showdown with Thorp. But it had been a lot of years since Ty had ridden anywhere on the vast northern sweep of Swallowtail. Time had dimmed his boyhood memories of the country. In order to avoid getting lost, he had set a steady but careful pace. As long as daylight held, he'd had little difficulty in picking out landmarks indicating the northwesterly way that should bring him to Lynchtown.

When the last of daylight faded out, so did Ty's bearings. The moon was bright enough, but everything seemed different by moonlight. He could no longer be sure of his direction or of natural features of the land once familiar to him. Yet he had no choice but to keep going. He was goaded by his driving, insensate rage at Thorp and by a coldly practical need to stay in his saddle. If he left it, he might never regain it.

Sometime around midnight, Ty had to face the appalling truth. Somewhere along the way he'd gone off trail, and now he hadn't an inkling of where he was. He topped a high bald ridge that offered a good vantage of the surrounding country, and that was no help either. Nothing in all that vast, moon-washed landscape seemed like anything familiar.

The sensible thing to do would be to wait for dawn. And he could use some rest too. But he couldn't risk getting off his horse. And his own stubborn rage fueled a determination to keep going.

Where had he gone wrong? Damn it, he should have thought to bring a compass! Ty tried to gauge his direction by the North Star. Had he swung too far west? He thought that was the case. So he would swing sort of east and then north. He would keep slowly riding that way until the first morning light brought him a renewed recognition of this country he'd known so well as a boy.

Morning came, and Ty was forced to admit that he was completely lost. He found himself in a stretch of heavy timber that rambled endlessly up one slope and down another. Badly out of condition, he was tired as hell. His legs ached unbearably. He had a canteen of water and a sack of grub old Diego Cruz had insisted on putting up for him, but he wasn't at all hungry. And he had to ration his water.

If he didn't get off his horse soon, Ty knew, he would fall off. And if he got off, he might never get back on. But Christ, he needed to rest . . . to sleep.

Cursing himself for being the damnedest fool under God's heaven for getting himself in such a bind, he chose a pine-bordered clearing with a spring-fed pool in the middle of. it. Then he cut the rope that passed under the horse's barrel and freed his legs. Ty dismounted. By holding his legs stiffly straight, setting his teeth against a multitude of aches and pains, he was able to unsaddle and water his horse, and hobble him out on a patch of grass. Then he spread his ground tarp on the needle-carpeted earth, rolled into his blankets and was asleep in seconds.

When Ty awoke suddenly, Sandal Cruz was sitting on his haunches a few yards away, tending a fire. He smiled politely. "*Buenas tardes*, Señor. You are all awake?"

Ty blinked groggily. He sat up.

"What the hell," he said thickly, "are you doing here?"

"I come find you. I been here an hour, but I think I let you sleep."

The sunlight was long and golden, slanting in flat rays through the pine boughs. It was nearly sunset. Ty had slept away the whole day. He groaned as he eased onto his feet and took a few tottering steps. Instantly Sandal was at his side, holding out one of Ty's own crutches.

"I bring this along," he explained. "I think you will maybe need it."

Bacon was sizzling in a skillet and coffee was boiling. Their fragrance tickled Ty's nostrils. Sandal had already cooked up a slab of bannock, and now he cut it in two and gave a half to Ty, who found he was ravenous. Unwilling to wait for the bacon and coffee, he wolfed the chunk of pan bread and washed it down with canteen water.

Between mouthfuls, he questioned Sandal. He couldn't believe the boy had trailed him all this way.

"Is nothing," Sandal said modestly. "*Abuelito* is a great tracker, and he teach me all I know long time ago. And Nate Drew, he track ver' fine too. Both of them learn me a lot. When I get back with doctor, *Abuelito* tell me to follow you up. He say he think you need help."

"Well, he wasn't wrong," Ty admitted wryly.

Some of the cramps had eased from his muscles; he felt sore but rested. Now he awkwardly seated himself by the fire, ignoring the pain of his legs.

"I wait till this morning," said Sandal, "and then I take up your trail. Is easy to follow."

"Unh." A single question filled Ty's mind, one that he dreaded to ask. "What did the doctor say . . . about Mrs. Banner?"

"He say she be all right soon." Sandal hesitated. "But you should be with her, Señor. Is what she need most. Will you come back with me now?"

"I . . ." Ty paused for a long, painful moment. His rage had blunted, but it had not abated.

Thorp. What about Thorp?

He put the question to Sandal. No doubt Thorp and the crew had returned from their nocturnal sortie against Lynchtown. What had happened there?

Sandal shook his head gravely, his young face troubled. "Is a ver' bad thing. They burn out Lynchtown. They drive the people away. An' the old man, Jack Lynch . . . he is dead. So is one who was his grandson."

"Damn Thorp," Ty whispered. "And then . . . ?"

"The crew drive the people off of Swallowtail and come home. They come riding in this morning as I make to leave. To follow you. But your brothers . . . they are not with them."

"What do you mean? Where are they?"

Sandal shook his head. He did not know. All he knew was what one of the crewmen had told him. It seemed that right after the raid on Lynchtown, Thorp and Free Banner had suddenly parted from their crewmen who were herding the Lynchtown people off Swallowtail land. It had come about quite unexpectedly. What was the reason for it?

All that the crewman could tell Sandal was the explanation offered by the boss. Thorp had said he was worried about Nate Drew, who hadn't returned from his investigation of the place where Larraldes had discovered Ike's body.

Previously, Nathan had told Thorp that he suspected foul play; he wanted to go over the ground himself, and Thorp had told him to go ahead. But Nathan's return was overdue, and Thorp was worried about him. So he and Free would go to check on him without more delay.

Meantime the crew was to escort the Lynchtowners across the boundary of Swallowtail and turn them loose, with a warning never to return under pain of death. That much they'd done. And that, the crewman had told Sandal, was all he knew about the matter.

"Is all I know too, Señor," Sandal said, almost apologetically.

There was a hell of a lot more to it than that, thought Ty. Thorp had always hated Nathan Drew's guts. Whatever had caused Free and him to ride off by themselves had nothing to do with Nathan. He added an uneasy qualifying thought: *Anyway, nothing good!*

As Sandal served him bacon and coffee and cold biscuits, Ty swiveled back to that thought with a mounting uneasiness. He'd been a fool to go kiting off after Thorp on his own. He had Serena to think of, and he could have a showdown with Thorp as easily later on.

But Serena was being cared for as well as could be. What about Nate Drew? Nathan was the best friend he'd ever had . . . and if that friendship had suffered neglect in recent times, it had been Ty's own fault. Besides, if Sandal had tracked him down so easily, couldn't he follow Thorp and Free with equal ease? They could backtrack to where his brothers had split away from the crew . . . and pick up their trail from there.

Giving him a curious glance, Sandal said, "What are you thinking, Señor?"

"I think I'm going to be a damn fool again," Ty said slowly. "Only this time you're going to help me. We'll start out first light tomorrow."

Thorp Banner was in a temper. It was raw and smoldering, held in check on a thin leash. He wasn't merely obsessed with a need to get his hands on Nathan Drew again. By now he was ready to kill him on sight.

When he and Free had reached the old trapping cabin where he'd left Nathan bound and helpless and under guard two days before, Thorp couldn't believe what he found. Claud and Sheb Purley laid out dead. Snake Purley trussed up as helplessly as Nate had been, and suffering from a slight gunshot wound.

Freed of his bonds, Snake was half out of his mind with pain and fury. True to his blood, he wanted revenge and he wanted it at once. Against Nathan Drew and "that goddamn breed girl" who had killed his boys. Thorp was hard put to get a coherent story out of him, but once he was sure of what had happened, he agreed with Snake.

Nathan Drew had to be fetched dead. And so did that girl, whoever she was. Sounded like she might be someone from Lynchtown. If she was, maybe Nate and her had headed for there.

But if so, likely they hadn't yet arrived when Thorp and his crew had arrived. Thorp had ordered the lodges searched before they were set afire. Of course the villagers, wary of trouble on Nathan's account, might have turned him away. Or hidden him elsewhere.

All this was guesswork, and Thorp wasted little time thinking on it. He needed someone who could pick up sign fast, and Pinky Miller was a pretty fair country tracker. Thorp swiftly rode to the nearby line shack to fetch Miller, leaving Snake and Free to dig a double grave for the Purley boys. By the time Thorp and Miller returned, the burying was just about done.

Snake drove a couple of crude crosses, pieces of cedar sapling cut to size and tied crosswise, into the head of the freshly mounded grave. He stood with his head bowed and his hat in his good hand, tears streaming down his gaunt cheeks.

"You coming along?" Thorp asked impatiently.

"You damn betcha I am." Snake's whisker-furred jaws barely stirred as he spoke. "You can lay ever' goddamn bottom dollar you got I am. Let's get a-going."

His red-rimmed eyes held a crazed look that

sent a ripple of gooseflesh down a man's spine. As they mounted and rode away from the place, Miller bending from his saddle to look for sign, Free ranged up by his brother's stirrup.

"Thorp, I don't know about this here," he muttered. "Getting Nate Drew out of the way, now that's one thing. If it's got to be, it's got to be. But that breed girl . . ."

"She's a witness, kid. We don't want no loose ends. Besides—" Thorp tipped his head backward toward Snake, riding behind them. "You want to tell *him* that, not me. She bagged one of them prize peckerwoods of his. He'll see 'em both dead if they don't get him first."

"Damn old loonie," said Free. "I don't like his eye, Thorp."

"Don't fancy it much myself. Happen maybe Nate or the young lady will shoot it out for him." Thorp showed his teeth, humorlessly. "It's them or us, kid. They're on the loose, and they will have a story to tell. We got to see it don't reach the wrong ears."

He would have liked Nathan Drew's signature on that quitclaim deed. But a likely facsimile of it might be forged by someone who was handy at things like that. Nate's name as signed by him appeared on several documents relating to the sale of horses that Thorp had found in the old man's safe.

It was soon apparent that Nate and the girl had

indeed made a beeline for Lynchtown. Once Miller verified as much, Thorp quickened the pace. It was late afternoon when they approached the village. Remains of the leveled lodges were still smoking; tongues of flame still curled here and there among the tumbled, blackened logs and lodgepoles.

High on the west cliff overlooking the valley, Miller found where Nathan and the girl had crouched, watching. Thorp felt an uneasy twinge, thinking of how, last night, he might have made a plain target for someone up here. It would have been a tricky piece of shooting . . . but even so.

Miller determined that the girl had gone down into the village and then returned. Afterward she and Nathan had departed the spot, and it was obvious that Nathan had had some trouble getting on his horse. Snake had said he thought he'd wounded Nathan, but wasn't sure how badly. Maybe, if he was hurt badly enough, this job would be a sight easier than Thorp had reckoned.

But tracking the two of them from this point onward was a far tougher proposition than taking up their trail to Lynchtown. Thorp couldn't puzzle out where they might have gone from here. Moreover, obvious attempts had been made to confuse their trail.

Even if Nate Drew was no longer in condition

to do so, the girl must have been canny enough on her own to make things a lot rougher for anyone who might assay to follow Nate and her. The trail led over stretches of bare rock and sometimes into shallow streams where no sign could be read until the horses left the stream. And then you had to watch damn sharp so as not to miss such places. Several times, Pinky Miller lost the trail and had to backtrack in order to pick it up again.

Darkness forced a halt. They made camp by a rushing stream and managed a sketchy supper off a supply of grub they had brought from the line shack. Then they caught a few hours' sleep and rolled out at first light to resume the tracking.

Miller took up the trail once more, and it was just as hard going as before. It led in a generally northwesterly direction, and Miller searched it out by painstaking degrees. But he was the only patient one of the party. Thorp was grim and tense. Free was palpably nervous. And Snake Purley was in a sorry state of mind any way you looked at it. He was wild-eyed and muttering endlessly to himself. He kept fingering the whip that was coiled around his neck.

The old bastard appeared to be losing his grip by the hour, Thorp thought narrowly. It would be well to keep a close eye on him. . . .

The morning sun mounted. It was nearly noon when the four men stopped on a rocky height that overlooked a wide basin of land where open, rolling meadows were broken by rambling ribbons of timber. All of them were perspiring freely under the hot blaze of sun. For now, at least, they were satisfied just to sit their horses and let a cool sweep of wind from off the mountain heights cool their sweating bodies.

It was now that Thorp, idly scanning the basin through his field glasses, caught sight of the two riders.

God, yes. It was them. Nathan and the girl. It had to be. They were riding across the basin at an easy pace. And they were headed right this way. Getting a tighter focus with his glasses, Thorp was able to fix the face of the lead rider in his sights.

Jesus. Yes. That was Nate Drew, all right.

Thorp lowered the glasses. He spoke with a quiet, wicked relish.

"Well, gentlemen. I think we have got a certain pair of people dead to rights. You hark to me close, now. Then all of you do like I tell you."

CHAPTER 18

It had come as a surprise to Nathan himself, getting out all that he wanted to tell Lolly while being hard to get all of it said in just the right way. He was a man used to locking his feelings inside himself. Maybe Horse Woman's coldness toward him had made him used to not admitting to anyone, even himself, a lot of what he really felt.

He wasn't sure about any of that. But suddenly and overwhelmingly, he was sure of what he felt for Lolly Hosteen.

Perhaps some of it was triggered by realizing that a girl, a woman, could have a genuine feeling about him. Sure, he'd dreamed his dreams. What man didn't? But maybe he'd never really believed it could happen for him. With a lot of men on a working ranch, it never did. You grew old in the service of one outfit or another; you knew the company of prostitutes on a town whoop-up. And that was all of your life outside of your work. It wasn't enough, and a part of your mind knew it. But you never looked for anything better.

Maybe, though, a man could get lucky. Nathan Drew figured he had fallen into a jackpot of luck.

Kind of mixed luck, maybe. Lolly Hosteen was no angel. She had more than a streak of pure cussedness; she was used to taking the bit in her teeth and running with it. She also had a quick temper that could turn downright vindictive when she didn't get her way. But too, she was like him in a lot of respects. She was a loner, fiercely independent and also fiercely loyal. She was his kind of woman in ways that nobody who followed all the rules ever could be.

Nathan wasn't sure just how to get it all out. But he said enough to make Lolly understand and believe. And he said it well enough to bring out a surprising softness in her. After that, for a while anyway, they had no need of words.

One thing for sure about Lolly Hosteen. Life with her would never be dull.

By late morning the two of them got to talking about what they would do next. Lolly thought they should either follow up the Lynchtown people and join them, or else take off across the mountains, get away as far and fast as they could, and make a new life for themselves elsewhere.

Nathan put his foot down flatly on both notions. This whole business had to be taken to the law. Predictably, that suggestion short-fused Lolly's temper.

"Godalmighty!" she almost shouted. "You must be crazy! I mean, just what white man's court is going to listen to a breed's word against a white man's?"

"I got to look for justice, Lolly," Nathan said quietly. "Ike Banner was my pa and he made me a legacy. I mean to claim it."

"Oh Jesus." Lolly turned away from him, throwing out her hands. "He's *serious!*"

Nathan's face grew warm under her sarcasm.

"Listen!" He caught her by the arm and whirled her back to face him. "It's not just the land or what it means to your people."

"*My* people?"

"All right. Your people and mine. But that piece of land is mine too, Lolly. Ike Banner willed it to me. Now maybe that won't stand up in a court of law . . . seeing I'm not a citizen, just a ward of the government. And neither the federal nor state courts in this territory have done much for an Indian claiming his rights. But *damn it!*"

Nathan's voice shook with the intensity of his feeling. Lolly looked at him wide-eyed; she said gently, "You're hurting me."

"Sorry." He let his hand drop from her arm. Now it was he who turned away from her, rubbing the hand over his mouth.

"Nate?" Behind him, Lolly spoke in the same gentle voice. "I never seen you get het up like that. Oh, you can be tough right enough when you got to be. I just never seen you get mad very easy."

"I reckon not," Nathan said bleakly. "Maybe

that's been my trouble. Trouble with too many of us. We keep backing off till we're in a corner. Then we got nothing left. I'm not backing off anymore, Lolly. I won't do any more running from anyone."

He swung slowly around to face her. "I'm going to claim what's mine under the law. Ike Banner owed it to me and he knew it. Sure, we got to be friends at the last. But that's not why he named me in his will. I'm his flesh and blood. He owed me. And I'm going to claim it, Lolly. For me. For you. For all those people Thorp Banner drove off."

Nathan hesitated, then said the rest of it. "And for Jack Lynch and your brother too . . . in a way. If you can't go along with me, say so. But somewhere a man has got to stop backing off. That's where I am at now."

She came into his arms in a rush, burying her face against his chest. "All right, Nate. It's what you say. You know, I been kind of a wild girl, ain't I?"

"I reckon you been that."

"Well, that's over. But it's a funny thing." Lolly gave a shaky laugh, her voice muffled against his shirt. "I think you got more of a wild streak in you than I ever had. . . ."

It took them only a short time to assemble their gear and ready their horses, and then evacuate the valley camp. They would head for the county seat on a route which would take them across Swallowtail range at a north-to-southwest angle, but swinging wide of Swallowtail headquarters. By now Thorp might well have men on the hunt for his half-breed half-brother, and Nathan meant to take every precaution against being picked up by them.

As long as he and Lolly held to timbered places, Nathan had little concern on that score. Both of them knew the country and how to move across it without being easily spotted. They would try to skirt around any stretches of open, rolling meadow, but here and there it was impossible to avoid crossing them.

At one particular spot, close to noon, they came on a broad basin made up of grassy stretches interlaced by narrow belts of timber. Here they momentarily pulled up their horses and gave the area a careful lookover.

"I guess we got to go ahead," said Nathan. "Just keep a sharp watch along here."

Lolly said tartly, "You figure you needed to tell me?"

They rode forward slowly, hugging the tangles of trees and brush wherever they could. Suddenly Lolly pulled her pinto to a stop.

"Nate," she said quietly. "We been spotted by somebody. I reckon when we crossed that big open place back yonder. I just caught a move off

in the brush"—she tipped her head to the right—
"over that way."

"Keep riding," Nathan said sharply. "Slow and
easy. Don't give it away. And keep your eyes
straight front, hear?"

At almost the same time he'd noted a stir of
movement among the pines off to their left. And
Lolly had been looking right. The people who
had spotted the two of them had spread out to
flank them and now were quietly working
toward them, holding to cover as well as they
could.

They wanted to get close enough to be sure of
their quarry.

Swiftly Nathan sized up the chances. Just
ahead of Lolly and him was a dense overgrowth
of brush that mingled with an outcropping of
granite ledges. As a place to make a stand, it
looked like their best bet. He couldn't tell as yet
how many men might be closing in on them. But
no matter what the odds against them were,
they'd have their best chance in whatever place
they would make the poorest sort of targets.

Quietly, as the two of them moved casually on,
Nathan told Lolly his thoughts. She nodded her
agreement without looking at him.

Just short of the rocks and brush, they abruptly
heeled their horses into a run, heading for the
nearest point of cover.

Even if the men stalking them wanted to get as

near as possible before opening fire, they were certain to do so before they thought there was a chance of their victims getting out of the open. Putting their mounts into an unexpected last-minute break for cover, Nathan and Lolly stood a chance of disconcerting their enemies just long enough to reach it.

They did.

A crash of gunfire came from each side, toward their backs, just before they burst into the first mottes of brush and quickly piled off their horses. By now the men who were after them were riding in full-tilt from either side, low against their horses' necks and cutting loose with their handguns at the spot where Nathan and Lolly had taken refuge.

They were so close all of a sudden that even in this harried moment, Nathan could swiftly identify all four men. Thorp Banner and Pinky Miller racing at them from one side. Snake Purley and Free Banner coming from the other.

Their attempt to take Nathan and Lolly by surprise had failed. Now they had no choice but to try nailing their prey by coming in fast and sudden.

Crouched behind an upthrust of granite rock, Nathan took aim at Thorp Banner and pulled trigger. But trying to fix on a moving target he pulled his sights too low. It was Thorp's horse that went down, pitching to the earth in an ass-over-teakettle somersault that might have crushed Thorp if he hadn't kicked hastily free of his stirrups and flung himself to one side, hitting ground in a rolling, bruising sprawl.

For a moment he lay stunned and unmoving. Nathan would have fired at him again right away, except that Free Banner was by now too close to ignore, bearing fast onto where he and Lolly were crouched, side by side.

But Lolly, coolly taking the time to make sure of her target, already had Free in her sights. She and Free fired simultaneously. As if he'd been struck by a giant fist, Free was wiped out of his saddle.

Almost in the same moment, Pinky Miller, coming in sight behind Thorp, swerving around and past Thorp and his downed horse, sent off a shot. Lolly had unthinkingly eased to her feet, making a halfway target of herself, as she'd fired at Free Banner. Now she gave a low cry and staggered backward. She dropped her rifle and then slipped to the ground.

Nathan was already bringing his sights to bear on Miller. With Lolly's cry still vibrating along his nerves, Nathan saw the brightness of Miller's red flannel shirt hang steady across his sights. And fired.

He sensed, with a rifleman's instinctive feel for a shot, that in the instant of pressing trigger he'd pulled a hair too far to the right. But his shot nailed Miller hard enough to spill him sidelong out of his saddle.

Miller's foot was caught in the stirrup and his horse, spooked now, angled away to one side in a panicked run. Miller's dangling body bounced loosely over the rough ground as he was dragged off into the timber and out of sight.

At the same time Snake Purley reached the rock and brush area, but he didn't try to rush the place where Nathan and Lolly were laid up. Instead he sent his mount crashing into the brush motte way off to the right of them. He'd vanished from sight before Nathan could even start to pull a bead on him.

Nathan remained in a tensely crouched position, his gun upraised, listening. But once Snake had hit the brush, all sound abruptly ceased. He listened a moment more.

Silence.

He looked down at Lolly. She lay unmoving on her back, one leg doubled under her. The shoulder of her Navajo blouse was wet-dark with blood and, maybe from the shock, she was unconscious. *Or worse!*

Nathan cupped his hand under her head, saying gently, "Lolly."

There was no response. Her mouth hung a little open; her head loosely rolled to his touch. But when he felt for her heartbeat, he found it strong and steady.

All right then. At least for the moment. But there was still Snake Purley.

Nathan rose quickly to his feet, rifle in hand. He would fade into the deeper brush where Snake had disappeared. There they could hunt one another out, man to man. Decide the issue once and for all. . . .

" 'Lo there, breed."

Snake's voice was a husking whisper, coming from a brush-shrouded wedge between two rocks nearby. Nathan froze, motionless now. His glance shuttled in that direction. All he saw was a glint of sun on pistol steel, and knew that Snake had him squarely covered.

He couldn't swing his rifle fast enough to break Snake's aim. And at this range, Snake had him sure-dead any time he chose to pull trigger.

"Tell you what, now." Snake's tone of voice was as sibilant as his name. "You bring your arm up acrost your shoulder and then you fling that piece o' yourn far as you can. Jest sail her off into the brush. Don't do nothing but that. You hear?"

Nathan hesitated only a moment. Obeying Snake's demand might buy him a few more moments of life. Enough time to . . . he didn't know what. But what else was there?

He was holding the rifle one-handed, and he swung it back and then forward and let go. It turned end over end in a high arc, flashing in the sun, and vanished with a crash in the brush.

"That done it fine, breed . . ." Snake rose out of his hiding place now. He parted the brush and stepped out between the rocks, his pistol pointed and on-cock. He halted a few yards from Nathan, his eyes livid with hatred.

"Fine for me, breed. Not for you. I jest wanted to get near enough to shoot you in the belly and watch you a-dying. Slow, breed. Gut-shot critter dies slow as hell if a man knows right where to shoot it."

Nathan's muscles tensed and gathered for a desperate lunge at Snake. They were too far apart, but it was the only chance Nathan had left. And he knew it would come too late, even before Snake jerked the trigger.

Nothing.

The pistol hammer snapped on a spent cartridge. It snapped again and again as Snake pulled trigger, wildly and futilely. Unwittingly, he'd used up all his loads in the burst of gunfire as he and the other three had made their charge after Nathan and Lolly.

Nathan did move now, but it took him an instant too long to unfreeze from his nerve-taut expectation of sudden and lingering death. Just a fraction of an instant, but long enough for Snake to drop his useless pistol and take several quick steps backward. In almost the same movement, Snake lifted off the bullwhip coiled around his neck and sent it peeling out in a dexterous crack.

The whip's popper kicked up a puff of dust inches short of Nathan's feet.

Snake was chuckling softly, a little madly, as he yanked the whip back and raised it again, poised. "You guard yourself straightway, breed. Won't do you a lick o' good, y' know. I growed up 'ith one o' these in my hand. I aim to pop out one o' your eyes. Then t'other. *Look sharp!*"

Nathan hesitated only a moment. Then his legs were driving hard again, pitching him forward in a half-dive, head ducked and one arm flung out as Snake brought the whip down in a ferocious slash.

The blow would have broken the bones of Nathan's face if it had landed on target. But it didn't. The lash curled around his outflung arm like a white-hot switch and spent its force in a whining circle of his arm.

Even in the agony of his savaged flesh, Nathan's dogged momentum carried him on, going down in his dive, his full weight catching Snake below the knees. Snake's legs were knocked from under him. With a yell he toppled forward across Nathan, who heaved upward in a single convulsive effort. It was enough to fling Snake to one side and flat on his back. Nathan scrambled across him, the whiplash still twisted around his arm. Snake had kept a grip on the handle. But enough slack remained in the lash for Nathan, in one savage effort, to loop it around Snake's neck. Then he yanked the loop tight— and twisted with both hands and all his strength.

Snake gagged and let go of the whip. He locked his hands on Nathan's wrists, trying to tear away his hold. When he couldn't loosen the strangling grip, he went wild. His wiry body squirmed under Nathan's pinning weight. His dirty nails gouged bleeding furrows on Nathan's wrists and hands.

Snake couldn't dislodge his enemy's weight. He couldn't get free of the choking coil of his own whip. His eyes popped; his face congested with blood and turned slowly to a livid purple. His tongue obtruded. His struggles weakened. Then his hands fell away and his eyes began to glaze.

Only then did Nathan relax his hold. For a moment he lay drained and limp across Snake's unmoving form. Then, doggedly and almost dumbly, he pulled the whip from around Snake's neck. It would serve one more purpose: to truss Snake up hand and foot.

In the fierce concentration of the encounter, he had forgotten about Thorp Banner. And now it was Thorp's voice from behind him that brought him sharply to his senses.

"That's right, breed. You come right on around with that whip, now. Won't do you a lick o' good, but you hold onto 'er anyway."

CHAPTER 19

Nathan turned his head slowly, wearily. Thorp was facing him from not twelve feet away. He had a whip of his own and was uncoiling it in his big hands. His shirt was dusty and torn from the fall he had taken; one whole side of his face was scraped raw, chin to temple. His big yellow teeth were bared in a travesty of a grin.

"Shooting's too good for you, breed." Thorp's voice husked and purred with hatred. "I am going to cut you to little pieces. If they's anything left o' you after, I will stake it out for the buzzards."

Remembering Thorp's prowess with a whip when they were kids, Nathan thought: *He can do it too!* He wouldn't stand a beggar's chance against Thorp, equally armed or not.

Nathan tried to prod up thought against the dull throb of his head. He doubted he could repeat the tactic that had worked on Snake—immobilizing his whip. That had been mostly blind luck. Even bare-handed, he knew, he would have no chance against Thorp in his present condition.

Slowly he unwound the whiplash from his arm and then maneuvered around on his knees, flexing his fist on the whip handle.

"Get up," Thorp said flatly. "Or I'll make mince-meat out o' you right like you are."

He punctuated his words with an outpeeling

swing of his whip. Its popper exploded the dirt a foot or so ahead of Nathan, snapping a sting of grit into his face.

Nathan lunged to his feet and whirled out his whip in an awkward blow that didn't connect. Thorp was already shifting sideways, easy-moving as a tiger despite his great bulk. His lash peeled out again. It ribboned across Nathan's left shoulder and upper arm. The burst of pain drew a hoarse yell from him.

He staggered back a couple feet. His shirt was ripped from shoulder to elbow; blood dyed it and ran down to the tips of his fingers.

Thorp could have taken his right arm out of action as easily—disarming him. But this was Thorp's game. He was taking a wolfish pleasure in it. He let Nathan take another cut at him and easily stepped away from it.

Then he struck again. This time the lash took Nathan in the right thigh. Nathan clamped his jaw against crying out, but a quick glance showed him, through a tear in his pants, a dangling flap of bloody skin.

Thorp was an artist with his weapon. Not waiting for Nathan to swing again, he whirled out three more cuts in rapid succession. Each one found the mark with a deadly accuracy—on Nathan's left leg, on his chest, on his right cheek. In seconds his clothes and flesh were covered with his pouring blood.

Through the haze of excruciating pain, he saw Thorp's face, ruddy and sweating and contorted. And suddenly he saw only that and his one thought was to smash it. He dropped the useless whip and stumbled toward his enemy.

Thorp's lash bit around his legs and circled them. With one savage pull he yanked away Nathan's footing and dumped him on his back. Shifting the whip handle to his left hand now, Thorp took three long steps and with an indifferent lack of haste picked up Nathan's fallen whip. He raised it, still holding onto his own lash tautly coiled around Nathan's legs.

Thorp shook his right fist, the whip held high in it.

"Take a long look at it, breed. It is the last thing you'll ever—"

The gunshot broke his words. And then Thorp was spinning off balance to the bullet's force. He took a wobbling step, tripped over Nathan's legs and toppled on his face.

Nathan used his last strength to heave partly upright and pull Thorp's pistol from its holster. Thorp was grunting and stirring feebly as Nathan rolled free of him and tore the pinioning whip from his legs.

Then he lurched drunkenly to his feet, hardly able to hold himself erect. He blinked his eyes and shook his head clear as two riders pushed through a fringe of scrub brush and into the clearing. They were Ty Banner and Sandal Cruz.

Sandal had an old pistol shoved in his belt. But the single shot had come from a rifle, and it was Ty who carried one.

Swaying on his feet, Nathan was able to say only, almost stupidly, "You."

Ty did not answer. He halted his horse and levered the Winchester, pointing it at Thorp, groaning on the ground. There was a chill, pure hatred in Ty's face that held Nathan shocked and mute.

"Señor," Sandal said very softly.

For a time-locked moment that seemed to stretch forever, Ty held the rifle sighted on his downed brother. At last slowly, very slowly, he tipped the weapon upward and fired into the sky. A kind of shudder ran through him; his fleshy face went slack and weary. He thrust the rifle out blindly toward Nathan.

"Better take it, Nate," he said quietly. "You better. Or I still might do it. Here. This too. Sandal, give me a hand down."

Ty palmed a pistol out of its holster at his hip. Nathan tramped tiredly over to him and took both guns. Sandal stepped out of his saddle, but Nathan did not wait to see him help Ty dismount or even to ask a question. He was already moving past Ty's horse, over to where Lolly was.

• • •

"So that's all of it, eh?" Ty said in a dead voice. "He wanted to get rid of us both. For the same reason."

Nathan nodded, watching Sandal build up a fire a little way from where he and Ty were sitting.

The day was waning toward sunset, and strangely Nathan felt ravenously hungry, in spite of a bone-deep weariness and the agonizing ache of his wounds. Sandal had bandaged his cuts as well as could be managed, and once they were back at Swallowtail, old Diego would do some expert stitching on the worst of them.

"That's how he told it to me," said Nathan. "Everything but how he sent Larraldes to take you out." An awkward pause. "I'm sorry about . . ."

"Serena will come out all right. She's young and strong enough and . . . I'll make it all up to her for . . . well, for everything." Ty rubbed a hand over his whiskered jaw, his eyes bitter and musing. "There's a lot to make up for."

Nathan glanced at him, but said nothing.

A wry, painful smile flicked at the corner of Ty's mouth. "Yeah. Even for the drinking. I can quit now. I made it through three days without the stuff. I had a good reason. And I've a better reason for not picking up on it again. Her. Serena."

Nathan's glance shifted to Lolly.

She lay bundled up in blankets a few yards

284

away. As he had figured, she'd suffered only a flesh wound, but the shock of a bullet tearing through tissue and nerves could lay a body low as quick as a fatal hit. The wound had bled cleanly and Sandal had dressed it. A little while afterward Lolly had come to. They had exchanged only a few words, she and Nathan, but those were enough. Now resting comfortably, she had drifted into a natural sleep.

"Reckon it takes a man a spell to find out some things," he said.

"It does." Ty grimaced. Sitting on the ground, he half straightened his cramped, aching legs. He was silent for a moment. "Free . . . he was in with Thorp all the way."

"Seems like it."

Free had been killed instantly. Miller had gone out in a worse way, dragged to death by his runaway horse. Both mounts had been recovered, and tomorrow the bodies would be slung across them and packed to Swallowtail.

Like Lolly, Thorp was not seriously injured. Sandal had dressed his wound too, and both he and Snake Purley were tied hand and foot. They would be taken back to Swallowtail. Then to the county seat, to jail and to trial. They sat with their backs against boulders and stared at everything except each other. Both men looked sullen and murderous, but neither had had a word to say.

Oddly, Nathan felt only a faintly bitter satisfaction in seeing Thorp Banner broken and defeated. For the same reason, he supposed, that he could regret Free's death: the blood bond of which he'd been ignorant for a lifetime. Another part of Ike's legacy and one not to be denied, even if two of his half-brothers had turned on him like wolves.

But there was a third one, too. And this one had saved his life.

Nathan looked at Ty's puffy, haggard face. There was a weariness in it that bordered on sickness and despair. No blame to him for that, after all that had happened. But he sensed an awakening strength in Ty, too. And knew that together they could sort out the tangle of problems that would face them in the days to come. Everything from the disposition of property to the future of Lynchtown.

And this seemed important. *A brother,* Nathan thought with a touch of unexpected pleasure. He'd often wondered how it would be to have a brother. Any sort of close blood kin that a man could truly care about.

As if reading his thought, Ty said, "Nate, we have got to do some real talking. There's a lot of things. . . ."

"Nate—"

The husky whisper had come from Lolly. She was awake.

Painfully, Nathan rose to his feet to go to her. He paused long enough to drop a hand on Ty's shoulder.

"We'll be talking," he said quietly. "There will be plenty of time for it now."

Center Point Large Print

600 Brooks Road / PO Box 1
Thorndike ME 04986-0001 USA

(207) 568-3717

US & Canada:
1 800 929-9108
www.centerpointlargeprint.com